"PLAY MERRY HELL WITH 'EM!"
LOU JACK HOLLERED

His men responded with a chorus of battle cries as they ran forward, throwing lead. The Germans flung themselves behind the ruins, spewing lead from their hiccuping Schmeisser submachine guns and thundering Gewehr-41 automatic rifles.

Lou Jack and two of his T-Patcher riflemen soon found that they were pinned down by snipers belching fire and steel from an upper level of the ruins.

Lou Jack fitted a grenade to his M-1 carbine, jumped from cover and dropped the hammer on the German sniper with the high explosive antipersonnel round.

But all of a sudden Lou Jack heard an ominous sound. It was the clank and whine and rumble that signaled only one thing: the approach of enemy armor.

As they dived for cover, the T-Patchers could glimpse the big Panzer tank and hear the shouts of the crack Panzer Grenadiers who supported the mechanized armor.

Every man among Lou Jack's unit knew then that they were all in a world of serious trouble.

A SHATTERING SAGA OF BRAVERY AND VALOR IN WW II

TEXAS

BLOOD AND GLORY
William Reed

TORONTO • NEW YORK • LONDON • PARIS
AMSTERDAM • STOCKHOLM • HAMBURG
ATHENS • MILAN • TOKYO • SYDNEY

At the start of World War II, Texas, with five percent of the U.S. population, provided seven percent of the nation's total armed forces. Its war dead exceeded seven percent of the total number of men killed in action. Twenty combat divisions were trained in the Lone Star State between 1940 and 1944, making Texas the U.S. Army's largest training ground. This book is dedicated to Texans who gave their lives in order to keep the flames of freedom lit.

If I have taken certain liberties with the historical record, it is because this book is not war documentary, but war fiction.—D.A.

First edition March 1991

ISBN 0-373-63401-3

Special thanks and acknowledgment to
David Alexander for his contribution to this work.

BLOOD AND GLORY

Copyright © 1991 by Worldwide Library.
Philippine copyright 1991. Australian copyright 1991.

All rights reserved. Except for use in any review, the reproduction or utilization of this work in whole or in part in any form by any electronic, mechanical or other means, now known or hereafter invented, including xerography, photocopying and recording, or in any information storage or retrieval system, is forbidden without the permission of the publisher, Worldwide Library, 225 Duncan Mill Road, Don Mills, Ontario, Canada M3B 3K9.

All the characters in this book have no existence outside the imagination of the author and have no relation whatsoever to anyone bearing the same name or names. They are not even distantly inspired by any individual known or unknown to the author, and all the incidents are pure invention.

® are Trademarks registered in the United States Patent and Trademark Office and in other countries.

Printed in U.S.A.

BOOK ONE:
D-Day

Salerno,
September to November, 1943

1

Red Beach, Salerno

Staff Sergeant Lou Jack Claymore narrowed his eyes to slits against the cold, stinging spray of the gunmetal-hued sea and bit down on the half-smoked stogie dangling from the corner of his mouth. He breathed the stink of diesel fumes as the amphibious landing barge chugged its way through clouds of exploding German flak toward the steadily growing line of a beachhead the size of a postage stamp.

The flat-bottomed, square-keeled Landing Craft Personnel barges—known as LCP or "Higgins" boats—had been specially constructed for the D-Day invasion of what the newsreels had dubbed "Fortress Europe." As the beachhead grew somewhat larger, so too did the conviction in Lou Jack's mind that he would probably die on this foreign stretch of sand, a victim of jagged German steel.

Like the other dogfaces of Easy Company, Lou Jack wore a sky blue patch on his right arm that bore the capital *T* that was the insignia of the Thirty-Sixth Infantry Division.

The insignia had earned the Texas division the nickname of "T-Patchers." Beneath the wreath-crested shield was the 141st's regimental motto: Remember The Alamo.

As an element of the Thirty-Sixth Infantry Division, the 141st Regiment could boast of a long and distinguished history of serving both the state of Texas and the rest of the Union to which it belonged.

Despite the fact that indigenous units of the division had been rounded out by conscripts from all forty-eight states prior to the Allied landings, the Salerno invasion was still mostly a Texas show.

Lou Jack's presence aboard the amphibious landing craft could be traced in a long line from his hard-fighting and hard-drinking, independent-minded, rough-and-tumble woman-chasing ancestors who had bled and died to make Texas free from Mexican rule and unite it with the rest of the fledgling American republic.

Squinting hard against the cold, early-morning ocean spray, Lou Jack clutched the M-1 carbine that he had made damn sure to know inside out and tried to will away the sound of death's beating pinions.

As NCO of Easy Company's First Platoon, Lou Jack knew all too well that his green, second-line infantry troops counted on him more than any other force, human or divine, to see them through the tempest of fire, steel and death that lay ahead on the Salerno beach.

Lou Jack was no water walker, but as the assault barge hit the surf just before landing and he watched the beachmaster's flashing red electric lantern signal the LCP pilot to land the craft and drop his load of men, he said a fast, silent prayer.

Too damn soon, the ratchet, clang, slap and splash of the armored steel landing ramp being winched down on heavy chains signaled the commencement of the assault. There would be no turning back now. The moment of heavy reckoning was upon the men of the 141st. The words of Lou Jack's prayer were suddenly forgotten in favor of a blue streak of impassioned cussing that erupted unbidden from his throat as he ran hell-bent for leather into the wall of flying German steel.

NO SOONER had the T-Patchers stumbled heavy-footed from the landing barge through the surf than stuttering tracer fire erupted all around them. Bullets whizzed from the German machine-gun emplacements commanding the high ground lying beyond the dunes that stood between them and safety, whapping and thwacking the surf and thud-thud-thudding into the mud.

Fighting the swells as they waded through the wave-tossed shallows toward the beach ahead, First Platoon stumbled across an obstacle path of submerged rocks more jagged than saw blades, slippery mud and buffeting waves that seemed to be weighted with lead shot.

The T-Patchers struggled to keep their wits about them against the blood-freezing knowledge that on the high ground facing them, German machine-gun and mortar emplacements of Field Marshal Kesselring's crack Sixteenth Panzer Division could rain death down at them from any direction they chose, for as long as they wanted.

The Germans had been planning their warm reception for a long time, spending the past few months dividing the beach into a deadly grid, making certain that every inch of sand was within range of their guns and their heavy mortars. Exposed on the open beachhead and vulnerable to attack from well-prepared enemy troops, the T-Patchers were scared witless as they hit the beach, spurred on only by the sure knowledge that there was no damn place to go but one: *forward*.

"Get on the beach! Get on the beach! Haul your fucking asses!" Lou Jack shouted at his men, shoving them out of the LCP and watching them struggle, first through water, then through sand, onto the beachhead. "Keep your goddamn heads *down!*" he hollered and roared as the first dogfaces out of the landing craft were already flattening on the slowly warming sands of the beach, facedown, rifles at the ready, just as the training manual had told them to do.

Others out of the Higgins boat weren't as fortunate as the few T-Patchers who'd made it that far. Already German flat-trajectory mortar bursts and automatic weapons fire had claimed the lives of many of Lou Jack's men.

As the last few troops out of the landing barge hightailed it toward the line of khaki-fatigued dogfaces scattered around the beachhead, one of them suddenly flung out his arms and gave out a short yelp as he plopped facedown into the sloshing drink, dead as he hit the water and buffeted to and fro by the action of the surf.

"Goddammit! *Don't look at him!*" Lou Jack hollered at the last men out of the LCP, who had stopped short to stare in shock at the lazily floating corpse of their former buddy, oblivious to the German rounds thwacking the sparkling waters with increasing accuracy with each passing moment. *The krauts have got us taped!* Lou Jack thought to himself then, his guts icing up as the hair prickled at the nape of his neck.

Lou Jack forced himself not to think about the dead GI and concentrated on the living instead, watching aghast as they tried to drag the corpse toward the shoreline.

"Move, goddamn you! *Move!* You lily-livered, gutless fuckin' wonders!" he shouted as he ran over and bodychecked the stragglers onward toward the sand.

Now he ran along with the other line-dogs with bullets singing around his heels as the pilot took the landing barge back out to the Liberty Ship anchored offshore, knowing that the mortarmen on the bluffs of Paestum high above the beach had got his range and that to hesitate for an instant was to attract the slug that had his name written all over it. Finally he hit the beach face-forward with his heart hammering in his chest and his lungs on fire.

From that point on, Lou Jack's orders were to dig in. And dig in Lou Jack did.

STRUNG OUT along the beachhead, First Platoon was every bit as vulnerable to German fire as each T-Patcher felt. The flat terrain—broken only by tussocks of beach grass and shallow swales—afforded precious little cover from the murderous fire cranked out by German 7.92 mm MG34 machine-gun emplacements.

Lou Jack wished he could stay where he was forever, preferably by burrowing down like a sand crab.

But he knew it wasn't possible. The blasted Army didn't draft sand crabs. They paid him to fight, bleed and die. All too soon he would have to either shit or get off the pot.

Already wave after wave of other landing barges were hitting the beachhead, sent on their short, dangerous journeys from the Liberty Ships that had ferried the troops to Salerno from Allied bases in Sicily and North Africa.

Wave after wave of fresh infantry troops arriving on the beachheads to make their lemminglike way toward the chattering German guns would force his men ever closer toward those flesh-eating bullets. There was no way around that fact.

"Newcomb! Front and center!" Lou Jack bellowed at a dogface lying about ten feet off to his left, his face buried in the grainy yellow-brown sand as he'd been drilled to do countless times. "Pull your dick out of the sandbox and gimme some commo."

"Yessir, Sarge," Newcomb returned, his voice steady but his eyes wide with terror. While Newcomb fiddled with the portable field radio unit that each platoon carried, trying to cut through the static to a clear channel to operations, Lou Jack took the opportunity to light up his spray-drenched stogie, which had gone out on the LCP, and took a quick look around him at the troops pinned down on the beachhead.

With the concentrated mortar and machine-gun fire hammering them relentlessly, his men were sure in some pretty shit, pinned to the sand with a mobility factor of zero. This state of affairs would prevail until the big guns on board the Allied warships anchored off the coast could zero in on the enemy and buy the boys on the beach some breathing space.

Just ahead of their positions, little more than a couple of hundred feet away, the man-high sand dunes gave the false promise of refuge from the incessant thunder of the death-belching German guns.

Lou Jack knew that his T-Patchers would have to reach those dunes sooner or later in order to stand chance-one of making it off this godforsaken beach. Beyond the dunes lay a series of irrigation ditches, and beyond these, the heights of the ancient Roman town of Paestum. There was a highway up there, and farmhouses that could be turned into defensible positions for an American command post.

But that real estate could just as well have been located on the far side of hell, which in a way it was. With no more cover than whatever was afforded by the shallow swales in the lees of windswept hummocks of sand and clumps of tall beach grass—and nothing else except open terrain all around them—any movement whatsoever was tantamount to suicide.

"Okay, give me a head count," Lou Jack shouted out. "Left to right. Let's hear you fuckwits sound off."

The head count showed Lou Jack that most of First Platoon had made it onto Salerno beach okay. Now he could believe that miracles happened to the pure of heart. Casualties, he reckoned, could have been far heavier.

"What the fuck's keeping you, Newcomb?" Lou Jack asked the radioman after he'd finished the head count, noticing that Newcomb was still hunched over the commo unit, seeming to take forever to get it operational.

When Newcomb didn't answer, Lou Jack frowned and tapped the kid on the shoulder. Still receiving no answer, Lou Jack rolled Newcomb over and saw the thumb-sized puncture made by a German 7.92 mm machine-gun round in the exact center of Newcomb's steel-pot helmet.

"Shit," Lou Jack cursed, using index finger and thumb to close the dead man's goggling eyes and smooth the death grin from his face. Then he snapped Newcomb's still-shiny tags from around his neck. Dropping the dead GI's tags into the pocket of his spray-drenched fatigue jacket, he grabbed the radioman's squawk box and began hollering into the mike.

"Valley Forge to Bunker Hill! Valley Forge to Bunker Hill...come in Bunker Hill!" he repeated, even though he knew there was no one out there to listen or care.

2

On another beachhead approximately a half mile east, code named "Blue Beach," Captain Murch Cody, commanding officer of Easy Company, lit one of the fifty-cent El Producto panatelas he'd brought along with him from the States and splashed through the shin-high surf toward the wave-lapped beach.

Right then Cody wished that he had brought along his Kodak Brownie, as well. He imagined that his gallant march up the sands would make one hell of a picture for the folks back home in Cook County, Texas.

Nothing was perfect, though. Especially when it came to the U.S. Army. Cody's assault barge was supposed to have landed at the other end of the beach. He was to have hit Salerno beach with the first of E-Company's units to storm Italian soil.

From the looks of things, though, Cody figured that he ought to consider himself a lucky man. He didn't need the reports coming in over the platoon's radio to tell him that there was a major bloodbath taking place most everywhere else, except here in the very spot where his men had made landfall.

All Cody had to do was take a gander through his field glasses to get the whole picture.

Cody ordered his T-Patchers to hunker down and eat sand while he reconnoitered the terrain. The line of dunes flanking the irrigation ditches lay dead ahead, maybe two hundred yards distant from their positions at the outside.

Beyond the dune line, Cody could discern the heat-shimmering outline of the barbed concertina wire that the Germans had strung on a formidable series of barricades. The barricades were made out of logs cut from thousands of local pine trees that had been bulldozed by the Germans to defend their forward fire positions.

A few stray rounds of small-arms fire and isolated mortar strikes were thudding home nearby, but to all intents and purposes, Cody's detail was well separated from the thick of the vicious fighting. The Hun just plain didn't seem to be paying his men much attention, and that was the long and the short of it.

"On your feet, you mother-lovin' heroes. Move out at my signal," he hollered, raising his whipcord-lean frame to its full height of six feet two inches, and pulling his Army-issue M1911 Colt automatic pistol from its regulation belt holster. He cocked the slide to chamber a .45-caliber ACP round. "We got us some goosesteppin' heinie ass to kick!"

Clutching their rifles as they sprang erect, Fifth Platoon made a ragged beeline toward the nearby dunes. Their combat-booted feet fought to find purchase in the shifting, granular sand of Salerno beach. Their fatigues were wet from wading ashore and their weapons were already fouled with mud and seawater. Any second, each of them knew, they could stop a bullet.

Cursing the Army, the Germans and everything else about their miserable fates, the T-Patchers of Fifth Platoon stumbled forward, suffering a fall for every few feet of ground they managed to negotiate.

"Captain!" one of the dogfaces, a redheaded private named Collyer, sang out suddenly. "You oughta take yourself a gander at this, sir!"

Cody noticed that his men were frantically diving to the left and to the right, each believing that his number was up, judging by the clamor of the shouts of alarm that now filled the air.

Suddenly Cody saw what Collyer was all fired up about. The German pillbox lay no more than a dozen yards from their position, just beyond a shallow rise in the beachscape, its machine-gun embrasure a dark semicircle against the sun-dazzled whiteness of the pillbox's front.

The low, squat emplacement of concrete was the color of the sallow beach sand. In the long shadows of early morning, it was almost invisible until one of the T-Patchers had stumbled practically on top of it, just as the Wehrmacht field engineers who had built it had intended.

Dropping down to a prone position, Cody studied the pillbox through his field glasses. The three-foot-long gun embrasure was dark, a toothless, emptily grinning mouth.

"What the hell are the krauts waiting for?" Cody wondered aloud. Not that it mattered much, though. The pillbox would have to be taken out if Fifth Platoon was to stand a snowball's chance in hell of reaching the safety of the dunes.

"PASS IT ALONG," Cody said to the nearest man. "We're taking out that kraut pillbox up ahead. I need two volunteers."

Expectably not a single T-Patcher responded. They had not been through basic training without having learned the first thou-shalt-never of Army life—never volunteer.

"I said I need two mother-lovin' *volunteers*," Cody repeated, running his eyes to the left and right and seeing nothing but averted stares. "Kilpatrick and Luce," he said next, unperturbed by the lack of enthusiasm demonstrated by his troops. "Thanks for volunteering. I'll put both you dingalings in for citations. If the krauts don't kill you first, that is."

"Gee, thanks a heap, Cap'n," they told Cody, their faces sullen.

Kilpatrick and Luce were soon armed with high-explosive phosphorous grenades and ordered to each take the pillbox from its blind ends on opposite sides of the semicircular gun embrasure. For his own part, Cody would draw enemy fire in order to give the T-Patchers a chance to blast the Germans out of the pillbox.

"Now!" Cody hollered as he broke and ran a zig-zagging course along the beach parallel to the surf line, snapping fire from his Colt toward the pillbox as he ran, expecting to be cut down any second by a hail of German fire spraying from the interior of the pillbox.

Nothing happened, however, and Kilpatrick and Luce had no trouble in sprinting around the back of the pillbox and dropping all four of their incendiary grenades directly into the yawning gun embrasure, belly flopping to either side as a belching tongue of yellow fire and a *crrrrr-ummmmp* of exploding white phosphorus and TNT signaled the detonation of the demolition charges.

After the smoke cleared, the T-Patchers cautiously made their way toward the blast-blackened front of the pillbox and peered inside.

"Captain," one of the T-Patchers declared at Cody as he made his way back to the pillbox, scratching his head and wearing a puzzled expression. "Looks like there weren't no damn krauts in here after all."

The pillbox having been officially declared taken by Murch Cody's Texas Army, Fifth Platoon was up and running again toward the high line of grass-topped dunes that had been their original destination. This time, however, enemy spotters had indeed taken notice of them.

Somewhere up beyond the dune line, in a limestone cave in the rocky escarpment of the Paestum heights, a German machine-gun detail was swiveling the stubby black perforated barrel of an air-cooled VZ37 squad automatic weapon in their direction.

The light machine gun was cocooned within the heavy frame of a tripod and equipped with a flip-up pancake sight. The spike-tipped legs of the tripod were anchored securely in the sand floor of the cave with heavy sandbags. Hundreds of rounds of 7.92 mm belted ammunition were at the ready.

The machine-gun crew had been alerted to the presence of the Americans by the sudden flash of their phosphorous grenades.

With a perfect view of everything that walked, lay or crawled on the Salerno sands of the beach below them—and the range to strike to the very edge of the waterline—the gun crew was perfectly situated to inflict maximum damage on the invading infantrymen.

The German gunnery spotter put down his field glasses and tapped the gunner on the shoulder. Fresh from the campaigns in the North African desert, where they had been bloodied in the heavy fighting in Libya and at El Alamein, the machine-gun crew still wore the pith helmets and dun-colored uniforms of Rommel's desert commandos.

"Now," the spotter said to the triggerman lying prone behind the deadly autoweapon. "Open fire."

Eddie Timmons, the son of a cattle rancher from Brownsville, had the honor of catching the first hit. A silver tracer round from the German VZ37 machine-gun cycling at 700 rounds per minute went in through his throat and sheared away most of the left side of his head, gouging out a fist-sized exit wound.

Brain matter glimmered for an instant as it flew through the air and splattered the dogface hunkered next to Timmons with quivering bits of red tissue. Timmons's corpse spun down to the sugar-textured sands, limbs still twitching and jerking without a brain to guide them.

Beside him, Chet Greenwell was hit in the groin, blowing off his testicles and most of his legs on impact. Ricocheting off bone, bullet fragments buzzing around inside his body made Greenwell's belly rupture a moment later.

Crying out his Maker's name, Greenwell watched his guts spill from his belly onto the tips of his boots, then collapsed face forward in a writhing heap, coughing up blood before he curled up in the fetal position and gave up the ghost on the cold yellow sand. Reacting to the sudden carnage, Cody shouted for his men to keep moving and not to stop for any reason.

Taking more casualties from the sudden barrage of automatic fire, the T-Patchers reached the foot of the dunes and flung themselves exhaustedly to the sandy ground at the dune line's base. Over the top was all there was left for them to go. Over the top and into the deep irrigation ditch that flanked the dune line at the other end.

"Up and at 'em, you goldbrickin', egg-suckin', mother-lovin' shitwits!" Cody hollered out above the ugly stutter of German steel, diving over the end of the dune into the fetid water at the bottom of the ditch. "Hustle! Hustle! *Hustle!*"

Suddenly the world convulsed in an orgasm of flame.

A German 88 mm shell—a stray shell dropped from one of the big guns miles inland that was carpet bombing the Salerno beachhead as more troops arrived behind Cody's men—exploded in an airburst just a few feet above the heads of the rest of Fifth Platoon as it crested the dune line.

The lethal blast radius of the airburst's twenty-yard concussion ring enveloped the entire line of scrambling members of Fifth Platoon, cocooning them in hellfire, saturating the killzone with a wall of razor-sharp, flesh-mangling shrapnel.

Those GIs closest to the epicenter of the blast were killed immediately, blown limb-from-limb like bullfrogs tied to firecrackers.

Arms, legs and heads, ripped from their sockets by the explosion, pinwheeled through the air. Unrecognizable chunks of bloody flesh that had been hearts, livers, stomachs and genitals plopped into the scummy water collected at the bottom of the drainage ditch like a red rain from hell. The mortified screams of mangled casualties echoed across the battlefield, and the air reeked with the noxious stink of high explosive mingled with the stench of rivering blood and lacerated flesh.

Hell had come to earth, but not empty-handed. It had brought a present for Fifth Platoon.

Death.

Those GIs closest to the bottom of the dune line almost made it to the safety of the ditches without suffering so much as a scratch. Most of the rest of the platoon weren't as lucky, though. In the space of an instant, the 88 mm artillery shell killed most of them and injured many of the survivors.

Seeing double, his ears ringing violently from the shock of the shell that had exploded so close to his position, Cody forced his brain to function in the aftermath of the battlefield holocaust. Everywhere the platoon's wounded were screaming, hollering, weeping, begging for help that was nowhere to be found.

"Morphine! For the love of Jesus, give me morphine!" The cry was repeated over and over again as the blast's echoes died.

"Captain! My guts are on fire!" came the sound of another voice close by Cody. The captain looked down and saw a T-Patcher named Quinn. Quinn's legs had been blown clean off at the knees. Quinn had a hole in his belly through which his intestines had exploded. They now hung out on the red-drenched sand, and the private was trying to stuff them back inside his ruptured belly. Cody sank to his knees, retching into the sand.

"Morphine! Cap'n, you gotta get me morphine!"

Cody had no morphine. There was no aidman to be found anywhere on the beach. Reluctantly he came to a decision.

"Easy, there," he said to Quinn as he slowly drew the Colt pistol from his belt and cocked the hammer. "Easy now, soldier." At last, moments later, as the echoes of a single shot died away, Quinn was out of his misery. Forever.

A HEAD COUNT TOLD Murch Cody that there were nine men left alive and not severely wounded. The rest of Fifth Platoon would have to be left behind. There was no other option.

"Collyer," he told the T-Patcher down the line. "You head back to the beach line. Find a medic and bring the pill roller back here. You understand what I'm telling you, soldier?"

Rogering that order, Collyer was already off and running, holding on to his helmet with one hand and clutching his M-1 with the other as he jackrabbited over the dunes and across the grassy hummocks dotting the beach.

Cody shook his head as he watched Collyer take off on his mission of mercy. He just hoped he hadn't sent Collyer running off to his death, but from the looks of things, his men were doomed to die here sooner or later anyway. Cody didn't hold out much hope for the poor suckers who'd taken hits, either.

"Captain! Look up there! Twelve o'clock high!" The warning shout came from a soldier behind him.

Cody looked and cursed. It was a German spotter plane, a slow-moving, low-flying Storch. At that very moment, he knew that the pilot was radioing back their position to the kill-gunners perched on the high cliffs beyond the dunes.

Even as the spotter plane disappeared over the dunes with a wavering drone, concentrated German autofire had begun to rake across their positions from two directions. Now Cody knew that the enemy had Fifth Platoon measured for a coffin.

Cody had no way of knowing that the Sixteenth Panzer Division, which was charged with holding the Salerno beachhead, was just as severely undermanned as the American Thirty-Sixth Infantry Division was ass-backwards in its execution of the assault. Half the armored defenses the Germans had prepared were unmanned.

The 88 mm shell that had done so much damage to Cody's platoon had been a lucky shot, lobbed by chance from the big railway howitzers that the Germans had deployed farther inland.

But the crack gunners in the pillbox who were catbirding it up on the high ground of the Paestum ruins had spotted them now and had tracked the punishing hellfire of their 7.92 mm weapons on Fifth Platoon's position. The Germans had murder in their hearts, blood in their eyes and the Führer's promises of world mastery to motivate them.

Poised on the brink of action, Cody stuck a panatela between his lips, lit up and dragged deep. "Let's get it the hell over with," he said to his remaining men, and charged forward into the steel-spitting German guns.

3

Spattered from head to foot with stinking canal muck, bruised and battered, their lungs full of choking cordite smoke, every last one of the T-Patchers of First Platoon felt lucky just to have made it as far as they had come.

The armed might of the German Wehrmacht had whittled Lou Jack's embattled troops down to a fraction of the personnel who had been ferried ashore by the landing barges to live or die by a roll of the dice on the killing ground of Red Beach only hours before.

It had taken them an hour or better to traverse the few hundred yards standing between them and the macadamized roadway that skirted the ruins of the ancient Roman temple complex at Paestum.

Now the T-Patchers were pinned down by the obliterating might of massed fire from German snipers positioned at the crest of the ruins and a mortar emplacement that lay directly ahead of them. They were forced to hunker down in the sandy scree like a clutch of prairie dogs hiding from a summer brushfire on the high Texas plains.

The T-Patchers had paid for every inch of Italian soil they had so far gained with the blood of the dying, the sweat of the living and the tears of them both.

Again the dogsoldiers of the Thirty-Sixth Infantry Division discovered with chagrin that they had their asses nailed to the shithouse wall by superior firepower. The enemy also enjoyed the tactical advantage of holding the high ground.

Lou Jack cursed the ass-kissers of Ike's joint chiefs of staff who had sent the T-Patchers charging straight into the blazing fires of hell armed with little better than water pistols.

By sharp contrast, the enemy was well equipped with automatic weapons and heavy mortars and backed up by Stukas and Panzers and reinforcements from Kesselring's Tenth Army, which could be quickly brought in as reserves.

The blooded veterans of Europe and North Africa, of *Der Führer*'s blitzkrieg war on Poland and the Axis conquest of the French Maginot Line, Hitler's minions at outpost Salerno were confident of their strength, freshly equipped and superbly trained fighting machines.

His own sorry-assed line-doggies, on the other hand, were green as north Texas pasture grass and equipped only with M-1 carbines, Colt pistols and the Browning Automatic Rifle in place of the light machine gun that Uncle Sam in its infinite wisdom had neglected to include in the weapons manifests, deeming it unnecessary to meet the German threat.

But, hell, Lou Jack thought to himself. It wouldn't be the first time that Texans had found themselves tangling with an enemy possessing all the advantages while they had none to speak of—except maybe the courage of their hearts and the steel-hard determination to win at any cost.

It probably wouldn't be the last time, either. Texans had succeeded before, and they'd do so again. Here. *Now.*

Lou Jack remembered the story that his pappy had told him about a range war his granddaddy had played a part in a long time ago. His granddaddy, a sheep rancher, and his men had found themselves in a similar position, bushwhacked by hired guns in the employ of the cattle ranchers who'd been lying in ambush for them at a remote pass in a godforsaken stretch of no-man's-land.

Way back then, his granddaddy and his crew had used surprise tactics to succeed against superior numbers and thereby turn the tide in their favor. Here at Salerno, Lou Jack's men would use the same approach to overcome the Germans in that mortar pit. Then they'd have themselves a look-see at that sniper in the ruins.

A COMBINATION of accurate rifle shooting and grenade strikes had at last neutralized the mortar pit, but there were still the ruins to deal with. Figuring that the last thing the enemy expected was an all-out, frontal assault, that's exactly what Lou Jack gave them.

"Play merry hell with 'em!" Lou Jack hollered. His men responded with a chorus of battle cries as they ran forward, throwing lead. The Germans among the ruins were surprised as those in the front ranks suddenly performed a morbid dance and colored the ancient columns with their spurting blood.

Their comrades reacted by dodging for cover and throwing lead from their hiccuping Schmeisser subguns and their thundering Gewehr-41 automatic rifles. From every direction ricocheting bullets spanged and pinged off the shattered stone ruins.

Lou Jack and two of his T-Patcher riflemen soon found themselves pinned down by snipers belching fire and steel from behind the cover of an upper level of the ruins, where a section of roof was still intact.

While the two T-Patchers drew the snipers' fire, Lou Jack fitted a 40 mm rifle grenade to his M-1 carbine. With the BAR men—men with Browning Automatic Rifles—blasting away from shoulder-fire position, Lou Jack jumped from cover and dropped the hammer on the suddenly preoccupied German sniper with the high explosive antipersonnel round.

Kahhh-booooom!

The sniper's death screams were cut off by the terrific explosion that hurled the other sniper from his crow's nest above the ruins and sent him somersaulting to the hard stone floor to land in a broken heap. Although mortally injured, the man wasn't quite dead yet. With a bloody hand, he reached inside his tunic and pulled out a mean-looking Luger automatic.

Before he could squeeze off a parabellum round, one of the T-Patchers bayoneted him right through the throat. The man spit up blood, went stiff as a board and then went limp forever with his head lolling to one side as the pistol dropped from his limp fingers.

"Nice piece," the T-Patcher said as he wiped the bloody bayonet on his khaki trousers, then bent down to pocket the Luger as a souvenir. Suddenly the soldier jumped two feet in the air and crashed to the floor on the other side of the dead German, the victim of a Schmeisser burst that got him through the rib cage.

By the time the close-quarters fight to capture the ruins had ended, most of the enemy were dead men. The few survivors lined up to surrender, and Lou Jack and his T-Patchers were surprised to see a couple of Italian troops mixed in among them. He'd thought they'd long since surrendered.

"The Germans gave us a choice," the Italians told the Texans. "Either we fight with them or—" He drew his forefinger across his throat by way of completing the sentence.

Lou Jack knew that the Italian troops could prove useful to the invading U.S. infantry forces. Since they knew all about the local terrain, they could be invaluable as guides.

As far as the prisoners of war were concerned, Lou Jack figured that the sooner they were rid of them, the better. Putting two of his men in charge, he sent the column of prisoners heading toward the U.S. positions back on the highway.

The sergeant didn't like further weakening his already understrength unit by two desperately needed men. As if that weren't bad enough, Lou Jack all of a sudden heard an ominous sound that he knew spelled trouble in spades. It was the clank and whine and rumble that signaled only one thing: the approach of enemy armor.

As they dived for cover amid the shattered columns of the ancient temple ruins, the T-Patchers could glimpse the big Panzer tank and hear the guttural shouts of the crack Panzer Grenadiers who supported the mechanized armor. Every man among Lou Jack's unit knew then that they were all in a world of serious trouble.

4

"American infantry troops, *Herr Oberleutnant*," the German spotter, a sergeant major from Innsbruck, informed his commander, a first lieutenant from Dusseldorf. "I make their position approximately one kilometer west of us."

The lieutenant nodded as he consulted his field map. It was spread out on the front glacis of the Caterpillar-tracked war wagon beside which he stood. His arm was wrapped around the barrel of the 105 mm cannon as the lieutenant dragged idly on an Italian cigarette, having long since learned to ignore its foul taste.

The platoon of American infantrymen would not prove very difficult to wipe off the face of the earth, he suspected. From all reports coming in from the beachheads so far, they were underequipped and green, second-line troops primarily from National Guard units.

The Allies were saving their best troops for the invasion of France that was sure to come soon. These men he now faced were merely throwaways.

The lieutenant was certain that the brief battle would be over in a matter of minutes. Then the squad of Panzer IV killer tanks that he commanded could roll unimpeded toward the beach and perform the mission they had been sent to carry out.

"Have the men spread out thinly," the lieutenant from Dusseldorf told his sergeant, flipping the remains of the Italian cigarette to the surface of the road. "Tell them to mass their firepower on the American positions—" he indicated two positions on the map with taps of his black-gloved fingers "—here and here."

"Jawohl, Oberst," the sergeant replied crisply, shouting orders to the Panzer Grenadiers who had fallen out on the side of the road beside the tanks while the lieutenant folded up the map, tucked it away in the pocket of his tunic and lit up another cigarette.

Climbing back inside the lead Panzer IV, the tank commander had little choice but to sit the engagement out. The elevation angle of the Panzer's cannon barrel was far too high for them to fire over the sights, howitzer fashion, directly into the American pocket. Tactically it was a job for the infantry troops attached to his tanks to handle.

However, the lieutenant ordered his tankers to man the Panzers' .50-caliber machine guns and provide cover fire for the grenadiers. The firepower might be wasted, but at least it would provide his bored tank personnel with some amusing sport.

"VALLEY FORGE to Bunker Hill, Valley Forge to Bunker Hill, we need artillery support, goddammit!" Lou Jack shouted into the mouthpiece of the commo unit's mike.

What came back was the same static and garbled requests for assistance from the hundred other units scattered all over the landing zone, causing a total breakdown in communications.

"The damn radio's no good," he cursed, flinging down the handset in disgust. "There's gotta be some other way of getting out of this chickenshit position. Got any ideas?" he asked the dogface beside him.

"Looks like feetfirst from here, Sarge," the dogface replied with a smile.

Lou Jack was of the same opinion. Without the capability of having the artillery boys drop a couple of shells on the armor that now confronted them, they were dead meat and every man knew it.

The Panzers packed enough firepower to blow them to smithereens without half trying. The only thing preventing the Germans from having done that already, Lou Jack suspected, was the fact that they couldn't get the right elevation angle on those big cannons, despite the fact that they were in a hurry to push toward the beach.

Lou Jack had little doubt that if nothing happened soon to break the stalemate, the tank commander would grow impatient and begin throwing shells anyway. The sergeant's train of thought was disturbed by the sudden appearance of a canal-drenched dogface, a straggler from another unit, who wanted to talk to the platoon leader.

"What's your outfit, soldier?" Lou Jack asked the dogface who had just arrived at the platoon's position below the Paestum ruins.

"Sixth Platoon, Sarge," the dogface said. "Looks like you got yourself some trouble with tanks," he continued, nodding toward the road.

"Yeah, so what of it?" Lou Jack asked the T-Patcher.

"I'm fifty percent of a bazooka squad," the soldier answered, waving to another man, concealed below the rim of the rocky overhang, who then sprinted toward their position. "Mike here's the other half."

Lou Jack looked over both men while he chewed on his cigar. It had gone out again after it had got soaked in the canal water, and the sergeant was waiting for it to dry out before attempting to get it lit again.

"Think you're good enough with that baby to keep the krauts occupied?"

"Sarge, I'm good enough to play the 'Star Spangled Banner' on this baby," he said evenly. Lou Jack could tell that the dogface spoke with pride and wasn't just trying to wise off to him.

"Okay," he said, nodding after a beat. "Here's the way I want you to play it."

MIKE AND SAM SET UP their bazooka position with speed and precision. Breaking out the firing tube and emplacing it on the rubble-strewn ground, Mike hoisted the bazooka onto his shoulder while Sam readied an antiarmor grenade from the ammo box containing a dozen others like it.

When they'd got all set up, Mike flashed Lou Jack the thumbs-up signal. As it happened, the bazooka crew had set up just in the nick of time, because the soldiers in the Panzer unit parked beyond the ruins had decided that they had stayed put long enough.

The lieutenant from Dusseldorf had instructed his men to move out. The commander's plan was to roll right up to the enemy's positions and pin them down with fire from the Panzer's front-mounted .50 caliber machine guns while the support team of Grenadiers hit the T-Patchers with automatic fire, mortars and grenades.

Now the lead Panzer was advancing slowly on the American pocket taking shelter in the ruins, the Grenadiers on foot behind it, covered by the line of tanks.

Mike tapped Sam on the shoulder, and Sam pulled the trigger of the rocket launcher, sending a bazooka round hurtling toward the lead Panzer. It scored a direct hit broadside, detonating with an earsplitting explosion and throwing up a dense cloud of choking black smoke.

At the same time, Lou Jack was off and running, a live grenade clutched in each hand. Shielded by the cloud of debris as another bazooka round slammed home, he succeeded in positioning himself just behind the Panzer, concealed by the pall of smoke from the burning tank and the clamor thrown up by covering fire coming from his troops.

The bazooka strikes weren't doing all that much damage against the heavily armored hull of the new Panzer IVs. Nevertheless, the bazooka hits had been highly effective as a diversionary tactic, enabling the T-Patcher to jockey into position to kill the tank the low-down-and-dirty way.

Hopping aboard the Panzer and yanking open the hatch, Lou Jack threw in the Mills grenades and jumped off as fast as he could. Behind him the tank exploded with a thunderous bang, belching flame from the firing ports on either side and up through the open hatchway. The Germans screamed within the hulk of the crippled German tank. Lou Jack was waiting with his eyes glued to the open hatch, which spewed great clouds of dense black smoke high into the air.

Holding his .45 at the ready, Lou Jack waited until the first of the enemy had managed to climb halfway out. The jack-in-the-box clutched a lethal Mauser in his hand. Lou Jack shot him through the face at point-blank range before he could fire off a burst, blowing off the back of his head in a syrupy shower of brain matter.

The second occupant of the armored vehicle was more sensible. He emerged with his hands up, shouting *"Nicht zum schiessen! Nicht zum schiessen!"*

Lou Jack motioned with the gun for him to climb down from the tank, keeping him covered every second. In the brief time he'd spent in Italy, he'd already learned one important lesson: never trust the enemy.

The lieutenant from Dusseldorf was only pretending to choke on the smoke, however, as he jumped to the shattered macadam. As he raised his gloved fist toward his mouth and pretended to be seized with a spasm of violent coughing, his other hand slid beneath his tunic and whipped out the small Polish automatic he had taken off an enemy soldier after bayoneting him some months before.

Pulling the trigger, he snapped off a few rounds at Lou Jack, but the eyes of Texas were upon him. Lou Jack's steely gray glance had never left the treacherous officer. Rolling under the line of sputtering parabellum slugs, he sprang to the "prayer" position—shin down, one leg tucked behind him—and let the lieutenant have five shots of Colt steel right in the belly.

The Colt barked out its knell of savage judgment, mean as a junkyard dog. One after the other, the slugs walloped home, spinning the enemy soldier halfway around and sending him crashing with a sickening, hollow thud into the armored flank of the burning Panzer.

The lieutenant from Dusseldorf slid down the big, red swastika that was emblazoned down one side of the Panzer tank, smearing the Nazi symbol with his fresh blood. He ended up in a sitting position with his chin tucked against his chest. If not for the spreading red patches across his chest and belly, he appeared comfortably asleep beneath the symbol of his beloved fatherland.

As the rest of the T-Patchers ran shouting their battle cries from the ruins, firing their Colts and Garands and Browning Autos at the stunned Panzer Grenadiers, Lou Jack wasted no time in jumping on board the burning Panzer and removing the .50-caliber machine gun from its pintle mount situated directly behind the open, smoke-belching hatchway.

Holding the heavy machine gun at navel height, Lou Jack poured a blistering hail of automatic fire at the oncoming storm troopers. As the heavy .45-caliber ACP rounds thudded into them, they danced a crazy jig just as their mighty Führer liked to do—except for the hot blood that sprayed and gushed from their bullet-riddled bodies.

Before long the enemy was practically lining up to surrender. The Aryan "supermen" had just been taught two things by men they had considered throwaways only a little while before. The first was respect. The second was fear.

The T-Patchers had learned a vital lesson, as well. They had learned that in this war, the only good German was a dead German.

5

Situated less than four miles from the beaches of Salerno, the railway junction was the last major terrain feature held by the embattled German army. The position was critical to the ability of the invading Allies to enlarge their tiny toehold on Italy into a full-fledged zone of occupation.

Even as Army engineers had begun to secure and build up the beachheads—bulldozing the sand flat to accommodate the jeeps, half-tracks and other mechanized hardware rolling off the barges sent from the Liberty Ships anchored offshore—German artillery spotters positioned in observation posts at the railhead had continued to direct shell fire from big guns inland, behind German lines.

Commanding approaches to the road, the Salerno rail yards included a scattering of low-rise concrete blockhouses and long, hangarlike warehouse units constructed of brick, in addition to the railway control tower complex.

All of these structures were infested by nests of German snipers. Heavily defended by a full battalion of entrenched Wehrmacht troops, the railhead was the final obstacle standing in the way of the Allied push toward more permanent positions inland from the beachhead landing zone.

The railhead had to be neutralized and secured, even though the German counterattack had lost its steam and appeared to be fizzling out. The artillery inland was untouched, though, and accurate fire was already slowing down the offloading of desperately needed war matériel from the ships lying offshore.

Because some semblance of order now prevailed—at least compared with the chaos of the first few hours of the Allied assault—the attack of the rail head was to be carried out with the support of Sherman tanks and howitzers deployed on the secured beachheads.

"SHIT AND SHINOLA," Lou Jack cussed under his breath as he spotted the bars on the epaulettes of the officer who was broken-field running from shell hole to shell hole across the fissured, rubble-lousy earth that formed a cordon between the rail yards and the highway ribboning off behind them to the east and west.

Lou Jack had recognized Easy Company's CO right away. Not that he had anything against Murch Cody personally, but the sergeant had been doing just fine, thank you, so far without the interference of officers.

All the same, it was only a matter of time before one of them showed up and started cramping his style with a lot of bullshit orders. Lou Jack supposed that he might as well be thankful that the officer in question turned out to be a T-Patcher rather than company brass from another unit, in which case he might just decide to go over to the other side.

"Real good to see you, Sergeant," Cody said to Lou Jack as he took cover behind the jagged hunk of concrete rubble that had once been part of a line of ten-foot caissons supporting an elevator conveyor line. With their typical precision, the Germans had removed all salvageable metal, leaving only the concrete and assorted fragments of twisted wreckage behind.

"How 'bout givin' me a rundown on your situation."

"The bars, Cap'n," Lou Jack told the younger officer, choosing to ignore his superior's question for the moment.

"What bars, Sergeant?" Cody replied perplexedly.

"The bars on your shoulder, Cap'n," Lou Jack told Cody, a finger-jab underlining his words. "The krauts don't like to waste ammunition. They'd just as soon shoot one officer as ten enlisted men."

Cody got the message pronto. Removing the bars, he tucked them away in his pocket while Lou Jack watched with a smile on his beard-stippled face.

"Now, about that report, Sergeant," Cody asked again, this time with an edge in his voice.

"It's like this," Lou Jack began, hitching back his helmet and wiping sweat from his brow. "We lost more than half our platoon back yonder on that motherfucking beach. We picked up a couple of men back there by the Paestum ruins, including a crack bazooka team. I don't have to tell you what our situation is right now."

No, Lou Jack didn't, at that. Cody could figure out the rest for himself. From the windowless concrete casements of the three-story brick warehouse building directly in front of them, German sniper fire continually hammered down on their positions.

Fortunately, because of the good cover provided by the line of concrete caissons for the hunkering Texans, the firing wasn't having much effect.

Of course, once the platoon attempted to move so much as an inch, the picture would change drastically. In the event the T-Patchers tried to storm the warehouse, they'd run straight into a wall of lead because the enemy had the field bracketed. Yet storm the building they inevitably would have to do. They could not continue to stay pinned down in their position indefinitely.

The only thing that had saved them from being pattern bombed by artillery so far was their close proximity to the German positions in the warehouse building.

The German spotters in the windows couldn't afford to risk calling in artillery fire that might cause a stray shell or two to be dropped on themselves, as well. They were meticulous soldiers and knew their only option was to sit and wait. Eventually their target would come to them.

Nevertheless, it was only a matter of time before the enemy got tired of playing cat and mouse and radioed one of their inland gun batteries to start dropping 88s on the T-Patchers' heads, or called in MEs or Stukas to strafe their positions. One way or another, survival dictated that the dogfaces strung out athwart the warehouse move—and move on the fucking double, Lou Jack told himself.

"Got any suggestions, Sergeant?" Cody asked Lou Jack.

"Our radio's busted or I would have called in the artillery boys already," the sergeant responded. "I reckon if we could soften up those krauts some, we'd stand a pretty good chance of kicking their asses."

"I'll see what I can rustle up," Cody replied, hollering for Fifth Platoon's commo man, who dodged sniper fire on a broken run toward the CO. Cranking up the set, the radioman succeeded in making contact with the artillery battery now in place on the Salerno beachhead.

The artillery boys promised to start shelling the warehouse right away. Unfortunately—though to judge by the way things had gone so far, predictably—nothing happened after a lengthy wait. On his next and final try, the radio jockey couldn't raise artillery again.

The hairs on the back of Lou Jack's neck were beginning to stand up in an allergic reaction to German ordnance he'd developed ever since landing on the beach.

"Sam and Mike, get your asses front and center on the double," he called out. The bazooka team hustled to Lou Jack's position right away.

"Set up your rig and get ready to cover our asses," he told them. "We're going in—with the captain's permission, of course," he added, turning to Cody, who had no choice but to give it. Lou Jack added that word was to be passed down the line for the men to get set to storm the warehouse as soon as the order was given.

This turned out to be a savvy move, because no sooner had Sam and Mike set up their launcher than a Stuka dive-bomber appeared overhead, screaming across the railway junction from the direction of the beach.

"Bandit!" somebody shouted. "Bandit at two o'clock!"

"Now!" Lou Jack hollered at the bazooka team at practically the same instant, just as a line of glowing tracers from the hawklike fighter-bomber stuttered down along the line of caissons, kicking up a hundred devils of dust as they impacted at better than 750 feet per second.

The sergeant's bellowed command was answered by the muffled *thuk!* and loud *boooooom!* as the 2.36-inch bazooka round burst from the pipe, traveled on an arcing trajectory for three hundred feet and slammed with a deafening explosion into the enemy positions in the warehouse, sending gouts of pulverized mortar and disintegrated brick in a dusty cascade that temporarily obscured the line of sight of the snipers who were holed up inside the building.

The combined force made up of First and Fifth Platoons was up and running even before the next bazooka round struck the building again, repeating Mike and Sam's devastating performance. The T-Patchers ran screaming their Hun-hating battle cries through murky clouds of dust, which also served to obscure the vision of the Stuka pilot, who fired off another long burst of .50-caliber Gatling rounds from his forward machine guns before flying off in search of better targets.

As far as the flyboy was concerned, his comrades in the warehouse were now on their own.

Through billowing clouds of choking blast smoke, the shouts and screams of men struck down by automatic fire from the windows of the warehouse echoed through the din of battle. Ignoring those who had fallen as they assaulted the warehouse, the first of the bloodied but undaunted Texas National Guardsmen gained the interior of the building.

Lou Jack was at the head of his troops, clutching the .50-caliber machine gun that he'd taken off the Panzer at the Paestum ruins. The heavy-barreled squad weapon chattered away, belching fire as it threw arcs of Krupp-forged steel back at its former masters.

Three of the defending gunners sustained immediate hits. The murderous volley lifted them off their hobnail-booted feet like scarecrows caught in a fiery whirlwind, sending them tumbling back to the shattered concrete floor as blood-oozing sacks of ruptured flesh and shattered bone.

There were many of the enemy in the warehouse. In the fierce close-quarters fighting to take the warehouse, floor by floor, section by section, it was hand-to-hand mayhem all the way. Rifles were useless when ricocheting rounds stood as much chance of killing your own buddies as they did the enemy.

Fists and bayonets were the savage order of the day. The Germans might have enjoyed the advantage since their training emphasized bayonet practice whereas the U.S. forces didn't. But by and large, the T-Patchers had learned how to handle a knife before most of them had properly learned to hold a spoon.

Pulling their long combat daggers from their scabbards, the T-Patchers fought with as much determination as their great-granddaddies had once fought the brutal hordes of Santa Ana's Mexican army of occupation. Texan against Mexican or Texan against Nazi, the outcome would still be the same: *Texan wins*.

Close enough to see the whites of their enemies' eyes, the ranks closed for the final confrontation. Lance Corporal Wolfgang Schmidt bellowed a cry of feral hatred as he lunged with his rifle bayonet at the throat of Will Tyler, a buck private from Lubbock, not even seeing the glint of the dagger that Tyler threw underhand straight into his belly. As the corporal keeled over, his last earthly sight was Tyler yanking the bloody knife from his belly and wiping it on his dirty boot.

Similar scenes were repeated all over the warehouse in fighting that was vicious and no-holds-barred intense, until finally every floor was secured. Only then did Lou Jack set down the .50-caliber machine gun that he had used to inflict such destruction on its former masters and lit up a fresh cigar.

With the warehouse now in Texan hands, those defenders who had not joined the scores of gray-tunicked corpses littering the bloodstained concrete floors surrendered in droves. Stripped of their weapons, they were made to stand with their hands clasped behind their heads and marched out into the rail yard, which had become an improvised holding area for German prisoners of war.

There the Germans captured by Easy Company joined their former comrades in arms who had been taken in other sectors of the railhead by American forces. Murch Cody and Lou Jack Claymore knew then, as they looked up into a sky now clear of Stukas,

Messerschmitts or bursting enemy artillery shells, that the conquering Germans were gone from Salerno for good and that men who cherished freedom were now here to stay.

BOOK TWO:
The Winter Line

Naples-Foggia Campaign,
November to February, 1943-1944

6

Monte Sammurco

The Thirty-Sixth Infantry Division's command post was situated in a building with peeling walls of ocher-colored plaster. Just a few days prior to the Allied capture of the town, it had housed the local headquarters of the Nazi Gestapo.

Before the changeover, the building had served as the mayor's mansion. When the Americans had moved in, their first task had been to take down the framed photos of Adolf Hitler and his right-hand men Goering and Himmler decorating the walls and to replace the German direction signs with English ones.

Now, with every last vestige of German presence removed from the CP, Major General Sam Hoagland, divisional commander of the T-Patchers, stood lighting up one of his ever-present briar pipes with an Army cigarette lighter.

Flanked by tactical maps on the wall behind him, square jawed and lean jowled, with cool gray eyes and a small, well-trimmed moustache, Hoagland looked every inch the spit-and-polish career military man. This he was.

A graduate of West Point, Hoagland was a career officer whose life began and ended with the Army. However, being the eldest son of an oil-well roustabout from Corpus Christi, General Hoagland also had a healthy streak of rambunctiousness in his character every bit as strong as the other qualities thirty years in the Army had instilled.

Taking a pull on the now sweetly burning pipe as he flipped the top back over his Army lighter, Hoagland heard two sharp raps on his office door.

"Come," he called.

"Howdy, General," said the young officer who now stepped through the doorway. Hoagland gestured for the officer to enter the big, Spartanly appointed room. Arriving to meet him was Captain Murch Cody, commander of Easy Company. Cody had received orders to report to General Hoagland a short while ago, just after his arrival in Monte Sammurco.

"Cody," the general began, throwing his arm paternally around the young captain's shoulders, "you ever hear the story of the Three Little Pigs?"

"Yessir, General," Cody deadpanned. "Learned it on my pappy's knee."

"Real good, Captain," the general went on as Cody lit up a Lucky Strike and took a seat facing him with his hands dangling over the top of a high-backed chair. He could tell that it was going to be one of those bullshit fairy stories that the general was famous for using to make his points.

"In that case you know how the First Little Pig, he built his house out of straw. And when that Big Bad Wolf came around, he could blow it to shit without half trying. Hell," Hoagland continued, "that fucking wolf might as well have farted at that old house of straw from way over in the next county and the First

Little Pig's house would have still been history. You follow me, Cody?"

"Sure, do, General, sir," Cody lied, nodding as he blew smoke from his nostrils.

"Now the Second Little Pig, he was smarter than Pig One, but only semismart. Pig Two, he built his house out of wood. Took more time, sure, but he figured it would stand up to the Big Bad Wolf a hell of a lot better than the straw Pig One used. Sure, Pig Two's house didn't make out any better than Pig One's in the end, but Pig Two had the right idea. His problem was that he didn't take it far enough. You still follow me, Cody?"

"Yup, General, sir," Cody replied, stubbing out his cigarette. "Sure do, sir."

"Good. Now, as you know, the Third Little Pig, he was smart all the way around the track. Pig Three got himself a mess of bricks and he built his own house out of them, and damn the fuck out of the other two Little Pigs who criticized him for being overly careful. As things turned out, Pig Three was the only one of all the porkers to be able to stand up to the Big Bad Wolf. Pig One and Pig Two turned out to be chumps. Pig Three had the last laugh on both of 'em."

The general spit a piece of tobacco from the side of his mouth. "See what I mean, Captain?"

Cody hadn't really heard a word. Trying to make sense of the general's stories usually was a waste of time. Cody knew that Hoagland would cut the bullshit and get to the point sooner or later.

"Yessir, General," Cody said to the T-Patchers' commander. "I think I see what you mean, there, General."

"Damn right you do, son," the general went on. "Here we've got us a similar case in point. The Germans—" he jabbed a finger at a black, north-south-pointing arrow drawn on the map between Monte Cassino and the Liri Valley "—are dug in here in an extended line.

"They've been building up for months. We know this area as the Winter Line, but that's a misnomer. Collectively what we've got here is a series of some six individual lines, the Viktor, the Hitler and the Gustav being the most heavily fortified among them."

"I read you, General," Cody replied as he nodded vigorously. Now he was beginning to understand what the general had in mind, and what it had to do with the fairy story he'd just been told. All the signs were pointing to shit-stick duty in a big way.

Cody didn't like the sound of what old Hoagland was building up to. His men had taken a terrible pounding at Salerno. They were in no immediate shape to move into another combat crucible. Maybe with a few more days of rest and hot food, but not right away.

"Good," Hoagland said finally. "Then you'll understand the urgency and the importance of the job I'm assigning you and your men, Captain. The Allied forces in this sector are just like the Three Little Pigs. The Germans, they're the Big Bad Wolf. The Brits and the French, they're Pig One and Pig Two. They don't think the krauts have got what it takes to blow them out of those hills, but I'm not so sure. We're Texans, Cody.

We're not going to build our house out of straw or even out of wood. No, sir, we're going to be just like Pig Three. We're building *our* house out of *brick*."

General Hoagland went on to spell out the name of the game. Cody and a selected platoon of his dogfaces were to undertake the task of reconnaissance duty in the rugged mountain country of the Aurunci range.

In seventy-two hours an Allied spearhead would be punching a hole through the Mignano Gap in the German Winter Line, Hoagland explained further. Allied regional command wanted a forward observation team to scout out the area and confirm reports that enemy activity was as light as had been reported by aerial reconnaissance before the final go-order was given. Hoagland made it clear that his orders had come down from the highest echelons.

"You'll have full artillery support if you need it," the general assured Cody on his way out of the command post. "You can count on us here behind the lines to back you up completely."

"Sure, General," Cody answered as he saluted the old man. That promise, he knew, was the biggest fairy tale he'd heard yet.

"One more thing, Cody," Hoagland said as the captain left his office.

"Yes, General?"

"Watch the hell out for the Big Bad Wolf."

"DON'T FUCK THIS ONE UP, Huey," Joe Crazy Face said with a growl in his voice. "You fuck it up, and I'll kick your maggot-ridden ass from here to Naples and back again."

Huey fumbled with the battle-scarred Kodak Brownie as Crazy Face tried to balance two naked, drunken women on his knees. The Brownie had saved his life at Salerno by stopping a bullet that would otherwise have gone straight through his heart. Even with the dent in it, the camera still worked pretty well.

The problem wasn't with the Brownie, but that both Huey and Crazy Face were as drunk as the women. Huey was having enough trouble just trying to focus his eyes, let alone the camera.

They had started out drinking grappa at one of the town's two restaurants, lulled into a false sense of security by its resemblance to white wine. But grappa packed a wallop like a Brahma bull with a prickly pear for a prostate. Not for nothing did the troops liken it to Kickapoo Joy Juice from the Lil' Abner comic strip. The knowledgeable drank it cut with grapefruit juice.

Before too long the two GIs had been joined by a couple of prostitutes. Bombed and starved by both sides, some segments of the population found that peddling flesh was the principal method by which they could survive.

The dogfaces had got used to such availability and accepted it as a fact of life. Anyhow, the girls seemed to enjoy their ancient calling and they weren't bad looking, either. Not long after their encounter, the T-Patchers and their companions were ensconced at the local bordello, along with most of the rest of Third Platoon.

"Goddamn you, Huey," Crazy Face hollered as his partner dropped the Kodak. "Now I am gonna kick your maggoty butt for sure."

Roaring like a bull, Crazy Face charged Huey head down, ramming him squarely in the stomach. Propelled backward, the two men smashed through the flimsy door and tumbled out into the corridor. As they tussled on the floor, doors opened along the narrow hallway.

Women in various stages of undress and their GI clients stood and stared at the wrestling dogfaces. Before too long the ogling turned into spirited betting, as money changed hands on the favorite to win the fight. As first Huey, then Crazy Face, gained the advantage, pummeling each other with ham-sized fists, the onlooking doughfoots began to fight among themselves.

CAPTAIN MURCH CODY pulled up in front of the bawdy house in a requisitioned company jeep just as part of a teak armoire came crashing through a window and landed with a splintering crash not a couple of feet from where he stood.

"You wait here," he ordered the jeep driver. "If you see any MPs, you keep them busy. Shoot them, run them down, I don't care what you do as long as you do it. Understood?"

"You got it, Captain," the driver told Cody, cocking his Colt automatic and holding it at the ready while he leaned against the side of the hood.

Murch shouldered his way through the growing crowd of onlookers that had gathered outside the bordello, most of them locals chattering away in Italian, accompanied by sweeping gestures of disapproval, and hightailed it up the stairs.

Cody took stock of what was happening in seconds. Third Platoon was a disciplinary platoon, made up of problem soldiers. But there were a lot of good trackers and land navigators in the unit. Lieutenant Rudolf Hooker had molded this motley crew into a crack unit. "Rudy's Raiders" had earned a reputation for guts and recklessness in equal measure.

Third Platoon possessed unique talents that Cody would need in order to pull off the hot potato of a mission that General Hoagland had dumped in his lap. Besides, few would miss these goldbricks if anything happened, the Germans least of all.

Hefting the Tommy gun he'd taken from the jeep, Cody pulled back the cocking lever and chambered a .45-caliber round. Raising the burp gun over his head, he fired off a long staccato burst of automatic fire.

In the cramped enclosure of the corridor, the Tommy's report was deafening. Some doggies who were drunk enough to confuse the gunshots with the sound of German artillery dived for cover. Others, drunk out of their faces on the strong local hooch, clutched their chests, believing they had been hit by the burst but were too smashed to feel it.

"Now listen up and listen good," Cody hollered through the clouds of cordite smoke produced by the burst of .45 ACP lead. "You eight balls got exactly five minutes to shag your asses out of here and form up like regular tin soldiers. After that, the MPs come charging in and you piss-ants get put on permanent KP."

"Shit, Captain," one of the T-Patchers put in sheepishly, "we were only having us a little fun."

"Fun's over, soldier," Cody sternly told all of them. "Your detail's been volunteered for a very important mission."

"What kind of mission we talking about, sir?" asked one of the T-Patchers, this time in a more respectful tone of voice.

"Well," returned Cody with a smile, "you might say we're gonna pull some hog fat out of the fire."

GENERAL BREMMERHAUSEN of the Fourteenth Panzer Division, commanding the German Winter Line, laid down his field glasses. He was unlike other German commanders because his practice was to regularly make unannounced inspections of the outposts and confer with his field commanders.

The Intelligence he had received from the Abwehr was less than worthless. Those overrated *scheissköpfe* put out only what they expected that the Führer wanted to hear, and the truth be damned. No wonder that his side was losing the war.

Bremmerhausen wanted the truth, and the Führer had a distinct aversion to that, as he did to most anything else that threatened his paranoid delusions of grandeur. And so the general broke with Prussian military tradition and personally visited his front-line troops.

Bremmerhausen entertained no illusions about Germany's chance for ultimate victory. The war in Europe was lost from the moment the Americans had entered the picture. That much was clear.

Now that Eisenhower had struck at the soft underbelly of Europe, it was merely a matter of time before the Allies marched as victors into the German heartland. Bremmerhausen did not want to consider the fate of the fatherland once the inevitable outcome materialized. To say the least, he suspected that the future of his country looked grim.

For the present, however, he was set to do his level best to perform his duty as a military man. His field commanders were well provisioned. There was sufficient ammunition, extra food and schnapps rations, and morale was generally high.

Here in the Aurunci, no soldier surrendered to the Allies in order to get a square meal, as had happened elsewhere, according to what he considered reliable sources. Because of their well-planned fortified positions, his Wehrmacht soldiers could conceivably hold out against the Americans for months.

Alas, that was the best that Bremmerhausen could offer his troops. Nevertheless, it was better than most commanders could boast at this stage of the game. Besides, Bremmerhausen had a surprise lying in store for the Americans once they tried to move through his territory. One they could not possibly expect and for which they would under no circumstances be prepared.

The Viktor Line

Rain was falling steadily at 0615 hours when Rudy's Raiders of Easy Company's Third Platoon took leave of their own front lines and advanced into German-held territory under cover of darkness and adverse weather conditions.

With the enemy's lines spread thinly along an extended front, and a thick pea-soup fog concealing their movements, Third Platoon could expect a fair-to-middling chance of carrying out their assigned mission of gathering forward observation Intelligence and making it back behind their own lines with their asses intact.

The fact that Third Platoon had representatives of the Choctaw, Apache and Cherokee Indian nations—men who could track an albino jackrabbit through a blizzard with the accuracy of a radar beacon—was guaranteed to increase the odds in their favor.

Apart from the Indians, in Rudy's Raiders comprised a bunch of ornery badasses who had grown up handling firearms, and whose great-granddaddies from the Texas *ayuntamientos* had faced off fearlessly against Santa Ana's men on that fateful day in San Antonio when the Mexicans had lost Texas for good.

In these men, the tradition of small-unit fighting that had been the deciding factor in taking over and holding the Alamo against vastly superior numbers—and had ultimately loosened and removed Mexico's stranglehold on the Lone Star Republic—had survived as a cultural legacy, handed down from father to son. It was a fighting tradition that was well suited to the nature of combat in the godforsaken hill country of the Aurunci Mountains of southern Italy.

In the Aurunci, winter set in early. The abrupt seasonal change could turn the rocky landscape practically overnight into a treacherous quagmire of slippery, sucking mud and driving, persistent rain.

There was virtually no flat, open terrain for men to maneuver in. Conventional tactics had no relevance in this high, rocky wilderness. Only small groups of men, acting independently, foraging off the land and using it for cover, stood any chance whatever of success in the sky-touching badlands of the Aurunci.

"Hold it there, Lieutenant," Joe Crazy Face said softly as he held out his hand. Dense mists swirled around the khaki-clad troops as Lieutenant Rudy Hooker came up. His helmet was pushed back on his head, an unlit Camel dangled from his lips, and he was porting an M-3 grease gun outfitted with a staggered box magazine containing thirty rounds of 9 mm ammo.

In the dense, swirling fog, the shapes of the other dogfaces took on unreal outlines. They could have as easily been rocks or tree stumps, or enemy soldiers looming suddenly, lethally, out of the enshrouding mists.

"What the hell is it, Crazy Face?" Rudy asked the Indian.

"Tracks, Lieutenant," Crazy Face answered, squatting on the ground and running his fingers lightly along the edges of the faint impressions in the ground. He lay down and put his ear flush against the wet muddy rock surface. "Don't hear anything now," he said as he straightened up again, "but it appears as though a column of men came by here not more than seven hours ago."

"Okay, pass it down the line," Rudy said behind him. "Look sharp and don't stray."

Conventional military wisdom held that it was dangerous to bunch up. But in the Aurunci, the wise abided by the direct opposite of this doctrine. Keeping together was the only way of being half-sure that a man didn't plunge suddenly over the edge of a cliff to meet his death on the jagged rocks below.

A couple of hundred feet more, and the platoon came upon a German gun emplacement. The machine-gun nest was built into a natural cave in the side of a mountain.

Signaling to Privates Crazy Face and Buckman, Rudy sent his two scouts to recon the cave. From their olive drab musette bags they pulled black Mills grenades and yanked the cotter pins with their teeth—any dogface in Third Platoon who couldn't accomplish this feat would have been scorned as a gutless weakling, no matter what the training manual said. The platoon advanced, holding the spoons tightly against the armed pineapples and the pins between their teeth so that they could be reinserted in case the grenades didn't need to be thrown.

The rest of the men watched the two scouts vanish into the swirling mists, only to reappear moments later. The pins had been replaced in the grenades, to be thrown another time.

"All clear," Buckman told Rudy.

"The kraut nest looks deserted, Lieutenant," Crazy Face added.

Rudy decided to have a look-see for himself. It wasn't impossible that there might be important papers left behind in the outpost, documents that headquarters back in Sammurco would want to examine. Reentering the cave with Buckman and Crazy Face, Rudy lit matches to see by.

The German position appeared to be recently deserted. The depressions in the earth looked as though they had been made by the steel baseplates of heavy-caliber mortars, maybe those big new 120 mm jobs the enemy had been using lately. A semicircle of sandbags still encircled the cave mouth.

Otherwise, there was only a scattering of miscellaneous debris left behind. The usual empty ammo crates, discarded field ration tins, pieces of newspaper and other refuse littered the cavern floor.

Having seen what he needed to see, Hooker ordered Third Platoon to move out. With the rain increasing to a steady drumbeat, the platoon advanced along the muddy trail that wound even higher into the upper elevations of the mountain region.

Suddenly, strange, threatening shapes loomed up out of the swirling mists and the driving sheets of rain.

"Crazy Face, check those out. Stoneman, Wilcox, you cover him," Rudy ordered in a husky whisper, raising his Tommy gun to belt level. "Now—move out."

They watched the Choctaw Indian blend into the mist and the rocky landscape like some ancient specter. Crazy Face moved cautiously yet quickly, using the uneven terrain features to afford him natural cover. In minutes he had crossed to the first of the many shapes that hulked out of the landscape.

As he came close, the Indian could make out the telltale outline of a tank. Moments later he was close enough to see the insignia emblazoned on their flanks. "Hot damn!" he swore softly as he stared at the Maltese cross of the German army.

RUDY DISPATCHED Private Buckman as a courier to the command bunker situated about two miles beyond the base of the mountain, just outside of Sammurco. There was no way he would trust Intelligence of this magnitude to radio transmission. He well knew that the Germans monitored everything and that there was a good chance the Hun would intercept any radio dispatch they made. It was too important a discovery to endanger.

The column of Panzers and Nebelwerfers—rocket throwers nicknamed Screaming Meemies by U.S. troops—weren't supposed to be there. G-2 Intelligence claimed they were located miles farther to the south, waiting to be used against the troops assaulting Cassino. Instead, they were parked here, just sitting and waiting, the last place on earth that anybody would expect to find them.

Rudy had no way of knowing that General Bremmerhausen had placed a Panzer unit in reserve to cover this critical approach to the Mignano Gap. His regular conferences with his field commanders had started the wily general thinking that the Americans might try to use this corridor as a possible entry route into the Mignano region. The wily wolf of the mountains would utterly destroy any little pig who chanced his way.

Right now all Lieutenant Hooker knew was that these main tanks and rocket launchers would clobber the advancing spearhead once it tried to punch its way through into the Liri Valley beyond. He hoped that Buckman would make it through okay.

PRIVATE TYLER BUCKMAN moved through the rain in a stealthy dogtrot, fighting the sucking mud every step of the way. He didn't see the foxhole in his path until he was practically on top of it.

Buckman was as surprised as the soldiers inside the hole were. Before they could react, the T-Patcher had used the razor-sharp bayonet on his Garand to cut the first German's throat. But the second one had already unholstered his Luger pistol by this time and pumped four shots point-blank into Buckman's heart with the adrenaline-fed speed of panic, killing him instantly.

Because of the booming claps of mountain thunder and the steady drumbeat of the worsening rainstorm, none of the men of Third Platoon heard the cracks of the pistol or suspected that their courier had never succeeded in getting through to Allied lines. Neither did the soldier in the foxhole, now rifling through Buckman's pockets, suspect that the lone soldier he had killed had been anything more than a one-man patrol.

8

Along the muddy ground, through the pelting rain, Ernie's squad continued to reconnoiter the terrain while the rest of Third Platoon broke out their entrenching tools and dug in to await the return of the scout patrol.

Sergeant Ernie Janssen was a big, rawboned Swede whose family had originally emigrated to Texas a century before via the wagon train route across the Great Plains. The two men he'd picked for his patrol were both expert trackers and shooters. Wade Hardee hailed from Houston, a short-haul trucker by profession. Billy Strong Heart was a full-blooded Cherokee and a well rigger in civilian life.

In addition to their Garand rifles, they carried extra allotments of hand grenades. They were also equipped with a walkie-talkie for communication with the main force of the platoon in its dug-in position. Because of the danger of interception, use of the radio was restricted to emergency situations only. Ernie's squad was code-named Able Tango, while Rudy's end of the operation was code-named Baker Foxtrot.

"This place spooks me out, Sarge," Hardee told Ernie as they moved cautiously through the operations zone. "Can't we just get back to the base and tell 'em what we already seen?"

"Orders is orders," Ernie snapped back. "Now zip your lip and keep your eyes peeled for krauts. I can feel 'em so close it's making the hairs on my neck stand on end."

Ernie didn't know how prophetic his words were. Less than a quarter of a mile ahead, there stood a stone farmhouse, its walls constructed from boulders cemented together for durability and strength.

The Germans had shot the farmer and his wife and taken over the house, fortifying the perimeter with concertina wire and barricades made of sandbags and still more of the local rocks.

The Germans were attached to the Fourteenth Panzer Division, whose tanks and mechanized artillery Third Platoon had stumbled upon earlier on their recon run. Despite their attachment, these troops were not regular elements of Fourteenth Panzer.

They were elite troops, members of the deadly Hermann Goering SS Division, commando forces ordered to the front from occupied France in order to bolster the line of regular Wehrmacht troops. The SS were mean and they took no prisoners.

"Looks like we might be in for a whole heap of trouble," Ernie told his two scouts as they saw the farmhouse materialize from out of the swirling mists.

From a position of concealment behind a jagged outcropping of boulders and a thicket of scrub pine, Ernie scanned the German outpost through his high-power binoculars.

The Germans had fortified the position expertly, he could tell. The farmhouse was encircled by a ring of rocks and sandbag fortifications, as well as barbed concertina wire. The cordon extended forward in a twenty-foot security perimeter in front of the entranceway.

Positioned behind the sandbags, to the immediate left of the farmhouse entrance, there stood a tripod-mounted Schwarzlose-12 air-cooled light machine gun, easily distinguished by its funnel-shaped muzzle that could spit 7.92 mm bullets at a cyclic rate of 400 rounds per minute. The squad automatic weapon was equipped with wide-angle sights and its crew protected by a curved plate of armored Krupp steel.

The surrounding trees and patches of scrub pine had been cleared away so that the squad weapon had a full 180-degree arc of fire, commanding the main approach to the farmhouse.

A soldier in a camouflage-patterned rain slicker squatted behind the gun like a ghoul on a gravestone. From the looks of him, he wasn't expecting trouble. In the slicker he wore for protection against the pouring rain, he looked wetter than a drowned rat.

"Don't tell me we're gonna check out that farmhouse, Sarge?" Strong Heart chimed in as Ernie stowed the binocs away in a musette bag.

"That's exactly what we're gonna do, Billy," Ernie told the enlisted man. "Besides, I hear they got Betty Grable held prisoner in there. The heinies got her tied to the kitchen table with her legs spread... Makes your head spin, don't it?"

"You're kidding me, ain't you, Sarge? They really got Betty Grable in there?" Hardee asked Ernie, his spaniel eyes glistening with expectation. The sergeant looked into Hardee's eyes and saw complete guilelessness reflected in them. Hardee wasn't pulling his leg.

"Forget that, Rufus Doofus," Ernie told Hardee, shaking his head. "Just get your butt on over there and scout out that kraut base. After we take a look-see, we make ourselves scarce and report back to the lieutenant. Saddle up, boys. We got tracks to make."

Minutes later, dog-crawling through the mud on their bellies, Ernie and Hardee had reached the outskirts of the farmhouse perimeter. Hardee might have been dumb as mule shit, but he was the best damn S&D man among the three scouts. With Strong Heart positioned with a BAR to keep a lookout for any patrols that might happen by, Ernie and Hardee crept closer to the enemy perimeter.

Ernie signaled to Hardee to reconnoiter the right flank of the farmhouse while he checked out the left side. Visibility inside was limited to a single first-story window set in the right wall. The patrol had that much going for them and not much else.

Because of the darkness and weather conditions, the squad could not be certain that a spotter wasn't stationed in the window, but they were reasonably certain that they had been unobserved. Had they been observed, their reasoning went, then the Germans would have shot at them by now. Unless, of course, the Hun was playing a game of cat and mouse.

Hardee cautiously crawled to just below the first-floor window, now visually confirming that it did not conceal a pair of hostile eyes. Gathering his courage, he slid up along one side of the window and cautiously peeked inside.

He had to remind himself to keep from swearing loudly as he got an eyeful of the interior. Hardee had never seen that many Germans together in a single place before. More than just this fact alone—the twin lightning flashes on their uniforms marked them as some kind of special goosesteppers. *SS*.

Having seen all he needed to, Hardee crouched back down again and dogtrotted through the mud and the rain toward the point where he was supposed to link up with the sarge. He found Ernie lying prone on the rain-sodden ground.

"Hey, Sarge! You ain't gonna believe what I seen in there..." Hardee began, but caught himself short.

Something was wrong with Ernie. As in *dead* wrong.

Reaching out, Hardee turned Ernie over. To his dismay, he saw that Ernie was now a corpse. Somebody had come along and stuck a knife in his guts.

Hardee jumped up in horror and felt something jammed into his spine. *"Hände hoch! Schnell, schnell!"* a voice barked, then repeated in German-accented English. "Hands up!"

"Fuck you and the horse you rode in on, Fritz," Hardee shouted, and raised his M-1. Before he could bring it into play, the steel buttstock of a Schmeisser subgun crashed with a resounding thud into the side of his head. Suddenly the lights went out on Hardee.

As the SS patrol detail carried Hardee's limp body toward the farmhouse, they did not notice that the bloodied corpse of the American sergeant whom they had bayoneted minutes before and left for dead was crawling through the mud in the direction of the outlying hills.

THE TABLE OF RANKS for the elite SS differed from that of the German regular army. In the Wehrmacht, the interrogating officer would have held the rank of major. As a member of the elite Hermann Goering SS Division, *Sturmbannführer* Franz Von Keltrop's rank had a more distinctive ring to it.

The same could be said of everything connected with Adolf Hitler's specially designated fighting brigades. Their tailored, night black uniforms set them apart from all other Nazi fighting units. They received special payment and other privileges.

In addition, they were entitled to wear the coveted death's-head insignia on their caps, and their officer corps were armed with the P-08 Luger pistol, as opposed to the regulation-issue Walther P-38 carried by German enlisted personnel.

Von Keltrop had begun his military career at the age of fourteen with the Hitler Jugend brigades in his native Munich. He had advanced quickly up through the organizational ranks, having proven himself the epitome of everything the Germans prized.

Cunning, ruthless and utterly devoid of mercy, Von Keltrop was the picture-perfect Nazi. He let his emotionless ice blue eyes sweep over the American soldier tied to a chair before him.

Inspecting the dogface, Von Keltrop could feel only contempt. The man was filthy. He stank. His physique was poor and his face oddly shaped. Compared to the German fighting man, he appeared to be lower than a mongrel dog. The second man they had captured was hardly better. Von Keltrop had no doubt whatsoever that this subhuman specimen would tell him everything he wanted to know.

"Revive him," Von Keltrop ordered the shaven-headed SS flunky named Mueller who stood beside him. Clasping his hands tightly behind his back, Von Keltrop stepped aside and watched Mueller proceed by bringing the back of his massive hand smartly up against the side of Hardee's jaw with the sickening, hollow smacking sounds of repeatedly pounded meat.

HARDEE AWOKE from a trip to Mars. The Martians all resembled Benito Mussolini. At first the Martians stood around him talking, but then they began getting physical, slapping his face and shouting at him in German. As his vision focused, he saw the faces of the Huns who were surrounding him. With a start, he suddenly remembered where he was.

"*Genug!*" Von Keltrop shouted, and Mueller's pounding abruptly stopped. The *Sturmbannführer* puffed on a cigarette and exhaled a long stream of acrid smoke past Hardee's face. Bending forward a little, he inserted the cigarette into Hardee's bloodied mouth.

"You now have the honor of being a prisoner of the German Reich," he began contemptuously, straightening to his full height again. "We are honorable men, soldiers like yourself. You will be provided with food and medical attention. We ask only that you cooperate. There is no dishonor in doing so. Remember that you are now our prisoner. By cooperation, you can only help to shorten the war for your comrades."

Hardee spit out the cigarette.

"My name is Wade Elmer Hardee," he said as evenly as he could, considering that his lips were swollen to the size of sausages and that he was scared witless. "My rank is private. My serial number is Five-Oh-Six-Three-Seven—"

The remainder of his sentence was cut off sharply by a fierce backhanded slap from Von Keltrop's gloved right hand that made him see Fourth-of-July fireworks.

"I did not ask you for your name, rank and serial number, *Du Amerikanische schweinhund!*" he barked, shoving his face in close enough for Hardee to smell the garlic-laden sausage that Von Keltrop had eaten for breakfast. "I have not asked you any questions yet. Do not mock me, or I promise you will regret the consequences."

"Go piss up a tree," Hardee told the *Sturmbannführer*. In return, he received a savage blow to the head from the Nazi with a barrel chest who had been standing off to one side.

Hardee did not know that his name was Mueller and that he was a former weightlifter from Vienna who enjoyed inflicting pain more than almost anything else in the world. Hardee only knew that it hurt like a regular son of a bitch. Raising his hand straight-armed over his sweat-filmed head, his face a sinister blank, Mueller whacked Hardee again. Over and over again...

After only a little while, Hardee got lucky. He blacked out. This time he didn't even see the Martians anymore.

9

"Hold your fire, goddammit!"

Lieutenant Hooker pushed down the barrel of Private Molena's M-1 carbine just as the dogface raised it toward the figure that was revealed in a sudden flash of lightning.

Rearing high, moving jerkily like a bad caricature of a monster in a horror picture, the figure finally toppled to the muddy quagmire a couple of yards from their foxhole.

"It's a kraut, Lieutenant," Molena said suddenly. "You should have let me pop him, Lieutenant."

"It ain't no kraut," Hooker rasped at Molena, swallowing hard. In the brief flicker of light, he'd seen enough to pretty much know who it was. The knowledge hit him in the pit of his gut like a hammer blow.

Handing Molena his SMG and telling him to keep him covered, Hooker crawled out of the foxhole and dogtrotted toward the position of the immobile figure. Mud covered the prone heap from one end to the other.

As Hooker had suspected, it was Sergeant Ernie Janssen. The big red blotch that stained the front of his olive drab field jacket told the whole damn story.

"Easy, there," Hooker told Janssen as he called for Lowry, the aidman. The platoon pill roller examined the bayonet wound in Janssen's chest and gravely shook his head at Hooker as he filled a syringe from an ampoule of morphine.

Janssen clutched frantically at the sleeve of Hooker's wet, mud-encrusted field jacket, waving away the morphine injection with hands that were scoured to the bloody bone from torturous hours of crawling across the rocky landscape.

His eyes were already glazing over, and his face was unrecognizable, caked with coagulated blood from multiple lacerations. His blood-caked lips moved weakly as he strained to utter words that he was almost incapable of speaking.

With the same fierce strength that had carried him an unimaginable distance over terrain as rugged as the moon's surface toward the platoon's position, Janssen pulled Hooker's face close to his trembling lips.

"F-farmhouse," he sputtered in a dying rasp, "...g-got Hardee and Strong Heart. A lot of krauts...SS..."

Janssen's eyes closed as he coughed once. Blood frothed from his nostrils and his mouth as his entire body shivered spasmodically.

"Janssen," Hooker rasped into the dying soldier's ear, teeth clenched in anger and determination. Ernie couldn't check out yet. Not till he'd said what he needed to know. "*Where's* the farmhouse? How *many* damn krauts?"

"Five, s-six miles west of here," he began again weakly, after the coughing spasm finally subsided. "Krauts...SS...don't now how many...." he repeated in a final blood-choked whisper.

Suddenly Janssen's body went into convulsions. His eyes bulged wide, threatening to pop from their sockets. The dogface shivered once, and his arched body sagged back down to the cold, rain-soaked earth of the Aurunci. He gave out a death rattle as his collapsing lungs forced air through his windpipe, and his heart stopped beating forever.

Lieutenant Hooker managed to pry Janssen's frozen fingers loose from the sleeve of his field jacket with difficulty. Almost tenderly he laid Janssen's hand at the big Swede's side and pulled his dog tags from around his neck, snapping the chain and holding the tags in his hand for a long second. They were stained with a hero's blood, and he let the cold rain wash them clean.

Then, dropping the moisture-beaded dog tags into the side pocket of his field jacket, he placed his thumbs over Janssen's eyelids and closed his eyes forever.

"Form a burial detail. Put him in the ground fast," he rasped at his T-Patchers through gritted teeth, knowing that a line had just been crossed.

Before this, he'd just been a line grunt doing a rotten job. Now it had got personal. *Dirty* and personal. Lieutenant Hooker was seized with a fierce anger at the Nazis who had done this to his men.

The gutless bastards who killed Janssen were cowardly butchers. Hooker would make sure those butchers paid the price they had coming. He would see them all in hell. Hardee and Strong Heart had to be rescued, too, assuming they were still alive. Now Hooker was sure that Buckman had never got through to command either with his urgent Intel. Since it was now a certainty that no reinforcements would be arriving to relieve them, Third Platoon would have to pull their own dicks from the wringer.

Blood and Glory

VON KELTROP WAS NOT a man to give up lightly. He would secure the information he needed from the Americans, who had so far proved intractable. They would talk, of course. Given enough time and sufficient motivation, any man would spill his guts.

Hardee was tied to a chair. Von Keltrop and his brutish enforcer Mueller had been pummeling him with their fists for what seemed like an eternity. By now he was more unconscious than he was conscious.

"I see that you are a difficult and stubborn man," Von Keltrop told Hardee. "Why do you refuse to answer my questions?"

"I told you there ain't shit I've got to tell you." Some of Hardee's teeth fell out of his mouth as he spoke. His combat fatigues were covered with an ugly mixture of blood, bits of broken teeth and dried vomit.

"I am sure you are correct," Von Keltrop said to him. "But that is a judgment that I alone can make."

The SS man signaled to his henchman. Mueller grinned broadly and evilly and lumbered out of the room. Minutes later he came back in, dragging Strong Heart, who was naked from the waist up.

The upper part of his body was covered with ugly welts from repeated whip lashings. The untreated welts were already beginning to fester and suppurate, as the Nazis had intended. His face was a swollen, almost unrecognizable mass of purple bruises, his eyes two blood-colored lumps.

"Stand this one up," Von Keltrop told Mueller.

Von Keltrop drew the Mauser pistol from the holster at his belt. He jammed the muzzle of the stubby black officer's pistol into the side of Strong Heart's head.

"If you do not tell me what I want, I will blow your friend's brains out," Von Keltrop said to Hardee in a matter-of-fact tone of voice.

"Don't tell him nothing!" Strong Heart hollered, gritting his teeth against the bullet he expected any second to come crashing through the side of his skull.

Hardee remained bitterly silent, weighing the alternatives. On the one hand, if he didn't tell Von Keltrop what he wanted, he had no doubt that the Nazi would blow out his buddy's brains.

On the other hand, he didn't want to give the son of a bitch the steam off his shit. Hardee didn't know if he could live with himself if he spilled his guts, and besides, he didn't really know that damn much to begin with.

"I am waiting for your answer, Private," Von Keltrop growled menacingly. "I will give you until the count of three."

Cocking the Mauser, Von Keltrop began counting down. Hardee remained stubbornly silent. Strong Heart shut his eyes tightly and steeled himself for the inevitable. His lips moved as he silently mouthed prayers he had learned in childhood but had never repeated since.

"Very well," Von Keltrop said at the end of the count of three, and squeezed the Mauser's trigger.

Strong Heart jerked forward and toppled in a heap onto the floor. Other than a hurt nose, though, nothing else was the matter with him. The hammer of the Mauser had come down on the firing pin with a sickening click. Von Keltrop had cocked the Mauser, but he had never chambered the round. The pistol's clip had been empty.

"We will try again later. Make no mistake—next time it will be no stage performance," Von Keltrop said with a laugh as he and Mueller exited the room. "Perhaps you will be in a more conversational mood by then. Until then, *auf Wiedersehn.*"

10

Proceeding due west as Janssen had told them to, Third Platoon located the SS outpost at the stone farmhouse without too much trouble. The T-Patchers hunkered on the rocky high ground just beyond its perimeter. Through his field glasses Lieutenant Hooker gave the German troop garrison the once-over.

From the looks of things, the base appeared to be undermanned. Judging by the activity level at the farmhouse, its SS occupants were at no better than platoon strength.

The outpost was on the alert, though, having captured American GIs, who in theory were not supposed to be anywhere near their positions. As a result, perimeter patrols had been beefed up. The rifle-brandishing sentries looked alert and suspicious. Being Germans, they were also tough and deadly.

Undoubtedly the SS had radioed Intelligence of the capture to their forward command posts. Yet no additional troops had arrived so far. They would pretty damn soon, though, Hooker had no doubt. With Gestapo investigators in the front ranks. As far as staging a rescue mission went, Hooker reasoned that it was a matter of now or never.

Given the state of affairs, Hooker had good reason to be thankful for the special equipment that his recon crew had been able to requisition through the assistance of Captain Murch Cody. The M-3 subguns were perfectly suited to the task of storming the SS-garrisoned farmhouse, and the extra grenades would complement the deadly SMGs quite effectively.

Apart from these weapons, each member of Third Platoon had another weapon that they could put to effective use: their bayonet blades, so much like the long, sharp bowie knives that their forefathers had used to similar deadly effect against Comanches and Mexicans in old Texas.

"Crazy Face and Dealey," Hooker whispered, turning to face his men. "Run the plan by me." He had made up a rhyme that even the likes of his goldbricks couldn't forget.

"One, two, three," Crazy Face and Dealey sing-songed in harsh-voiced unison, *"the sentries are history."*

"Four, five, six," Flagg, Burnside and Molena continued, reciting their part of the rhyme, *"the left side of the farmhouse gets nixed."*

"Seven, eight, nine," Stoneman and Hood intoned finally, *"the lieutenant and us come in the front door to snuff out the Nazi slime."*

"Fucking-A," Hooker said, nodding his approval. "Any further questions from you dingalings?"

Lieutenant Hooker was pleased to note that there weren't any.

THE HUNT WAS IN Joe Crazy Face's blood; like a skill that's never forgotten, it was always there, ready to be called upon when needed. The crackle of rain on soil and the background rumble of mountain thunder provided perfect cover as he crept up behind the SS sentry walking his perimeter.

The rest happened just like the GI training manual spelled it out.

Gripping the knife in his right hand, thumb down on the haft to maintain an even pressure, Crazy Face gripped the Nazi over the mouth and nose hard, jerking the head backward while raising the knife hand high.

Maintaining the tight grip over the man's nose and mouth to stifle any scream, Crazy Face plunged the bayonet in just beneath the right ear and twisted it, scrambling the Nazi's brains and feeling the kill instantly go limp.

Looking from side to side as he lowered the dead sentry to the muddy earth, Crazy Face dragged the corpse behind the concealment of some stacked bales of hay where he wouldn't be noticed for awhile.

Cleaning the knife on the German's field gray uniform, he replaced it in its sheath and raised his M-3 SMG, a full 30-round ammo clip in its receiver and a 9 mm round already chambered. Retracting its wire buttstock, he clamped it securely under his right armpit and checked his watch.

Private Joe Crazy Face was right on schedule.

Just as this was happening, Dealey had accomplished the same objective as Crazy Face had, albeit with a little more difficulty. Dealey had hesitated a moment too long before sticking the SS patrol, and his Nazi managed to struggle free, face livid and eyes wide with terror.

Dealey was forced to throw the knife underhand, scoring a perfect bull's-eye on the exposed throat. As the SS soldier reached for the knife and tried to pull it out of his blood-spurting trachea, Dealey tackled the doomed man and clubbed him to death with repeated smashes of his SMG buttstock until the Nazi went limp and motionless.

Crouching beside the now brutally battered corpse and breathing heavily from the exertion of the death struggle, Dealey glanced furtively from side to side, checking for any indications that the struggle had been observed.

But luck and the weather were on his side. None of the other perimeter patrols had heard a thing. Cleaning the bloody bayonet knife on the dead German's uniform and replacing it in its sheath, Dealey also fisted his special-issue SMG and moved stealthily toward the garrison.

"ON MY SIGNAL!" Hooker said to his T-Patchers. As they all pitched offensive Mills grenades at the sandbag-ringed Schwarzlose gun pit, they sprinted forward, hoping that the sentries had been taken out according to plan and that the other squads were moving in from their respective ends of the farmhouse.

Twin cracks of exploding grenades above the noise of the driving rain signaled the commencement of the T-Patchers' surprise attack. Expertly pitched, the two grenades kayoed the lone German gunner in the Schwarzlose machine-gun emplacement guarding the entrance to the farmhouse, hurling his shattered body over the sandbags to lie in a broken heap on the muddy ground.

The ugly chatter of Schmeisser fire joined the howling chorus of death as sentries in a half-tracked patrol car stationed nearby opened up with their MP-40 SMGs. Hooker, Stoneman and Hood answered the autofire, snapping off defensive bursts of 9 mm M-3 rounds to the left and the right as they zigzagged through the cordite smoke of the detonated grenades.

Riddled by Yank parabellums, the Germans in the half-track threw up their hands and jerked like a trio of out-of-control marionettes. Snapping a Mills grenade from shoulder webbing, Stoneman lobbed another pineapple into the staff car and was rewarded by a ballooning pillar of incinerating fire as the gas tank exploded.

Making their approaches from the left and right of the farmhouse, strike teams one and two pitched grenades of their own and poured SMG fire at the Germans as Hooker and members of squad three flattened in a line on either side of the farmhouse door, hands clutching ready-to-throw grenades.

At Hooker's nod, the waffle-surfaced Mills bombs were tossed inside the doorway. Hitting the floor with hollow thuds, they bounced, rolled and went off with almost simultaneous reports. The combined blast shook the ground, and squad three heard the fresh screams of dying Germans rip the air just below the thunder of the two multiple grenade explosions.

"Cover me!" Hooker roared, and went into the farmhouse on a crouch. Holding his M-3 grease gun at hip level, he hosed down the interior with blazing parabellum steel as he whipped the SMG from side to side with a grimace on his face and murder in his heart. More Germans died in a bullet-riddled dance, already wounded and dazed from the grenade explosions that had preceded the murderous autofire.

As team three entered the rooms beyond the farmhouse kitchen, with the other two strike teams right behind them, Mueller jumped out from hiding. Cradled in his massive, tattooed arms was a Knorr-Bremse MG 35/36 light machine-gun, looking like a toy in those beefy hands. The 7.92 mm belts dangling from it packed hundreds of rounds of firepower. The bullets it fired were all too real.

"Goddamn you Americans!" Mueller hollered as he cut loose with a withering hail of fire, hitting Stoneman and blowing most of his heart region away in a glittering spray of red and catapulting the corpse over a nearby chair. The onrushing T-Patchers had no choice but to dive for cover. As Hood ducked for cover, he struck his head on the edge of the kitchen stove and was knocked cold.

Upending the massive oaken front of the kitchen table, Hooker used it as a makeshift shield. The heavy caliber 7.92s whined as they thudded into the table by the score, their impact neutralized to some extent by the dense wood from which it was fashioned.

Hooker lobbed a grenade from behind the tenuous cover of the table, but Mueller still kept firing the flame-belching Knorr-Bremse, his head thrown back in obscene exultation. He rocked back on his heels, but was otherwise unhurt by the exploding grenade.

"I come for you, *Schweinhund!*" Mueller shrieked with a demented laugh, jerking the trigger. "Soon I take you to meet *Der Teufel!*"

The maniacally laughing Nazi poured on the fire and the bullets were beginning to take their inevitable toll as the tabletop disintegrated under the steady onslaught. Realizing that there would soon be nothing left to use as a shield, Hooker knew he had to make his play damn soon. Despite the long survival odds, staying put was suicide.

Pulling a fresh SMG clip from a mag pouch on his web belt, Hooker reloaded his M-3 and jumped out, spitting autofire at Mueller. Mueller was knocked back on his heels by the hail of parabellums, spurting blood from a dozen puncture wounds across his upper chest, but amazingly the indestructible German continued to keep on firing the big machine gun.

Mueller bellowed again as he tracked the smoking barrel of the Knorr-Bremse MG across the room, realizing now that he was out of ammo.

"You are as good as dead! I am taking you to hell with me!" Mueller continued, throwing down the now useless Knorr-Bremse and pulling two StG-24 "potato masher" stick grenades from his belt and arming them with tugs on the pull-strings in their wooden handles.

Head down, he charged the Americans, bellowing like a bull. Hooker and Dealey managed to dive out of harm's way, but Burnside wasn't fast enough to evade the massively built Nazi juggernaut. Bearing down on Burnside like a steamroller, Mueller easily bowled the T-Patcher over.

Kuhhhh-blammmm!

The German and Burnside were both blown to mincemeat-sized pieces by the combined force of the walloping explosion. Hooker hollered for his surviving men to follow him into the next room. There was nothing they could do for Burnside except notify graves registration.

In the basement of the farmhouse, the T-Patchers came to a heavy wooden door. The door apparently was bolted from the inside. Hooker stood back and blew it clean off its hinges with a single grenade sent rolling toward it.

"Stay where you are!" they heard a German-accented voice command shrilly as they went inside moments later. In the clearing smoke, Hooker and his men of Third Platoon saw SS *Sturmbannführer* Von Keltrop covering Strong Heart and Hardee with a Mauser machine pistol.

Strong Heart appeared to be unconscious, and Hardee wasn't in much better shape. The Mauser in the Nazi's gloved fist waved from the head of one man to the other, malignantly glinting like some black, venomous snake.

"We got you cold, German," Hooker snarled at the SS officer, keeping his SMG trained on him. "The rest of your fancy SS heinies are now playing patty-cake with the Valkyries. Throw down the gun. *Machen zu* with the hands up."

"Do not toy with me, you insolent bag of piss," snapped Von Keltrop. "I still hold the gun on your comrades. I assure you that I will take them both with me should you be foolish enough to shoot."

"Don't think so, shithead," Hooker growled, firing a well-placed 9 mm SMG round into the Nazi's hand. The Mauser flew from his grasp as he let out a pathetic howl and slumped in agony to the floor, minus most of his fingers.

Stunned, the Nazi lay trembling like a beaten mutt. He hadn't counted on meeting up with men who'd handled a gun before they were weaned on mother's milk. Such a display of marksmanship, Von Keltrop thought to his chagrin, was nothing short of unbelievable.

"Frisk the heinie creep," Hooker ordered Dealey as he unscabbarded his knife and cut Strong Heart and Hardee loose. Hardee was shaky, but he was at least in good enough shape to walk.

Strong Heart was in no condition to move at all, however. The pill roller said that he might be brain-damaged from the severe beating he'd taken. Hooker ordered his men to tear a door off its hinges and use it as a stretcher for the injured private. Then he sent out squads to scout out the garrison for anything of value to either the Intelligence boys or themselves.

"What are we gonna do about ol' Fritz here, Lieutenant?" one of the T-Patchers asked, eyeing the SS man with a diabolical light as he drew his bayonet knife and ran his finger over its razor-sharp cutting edge.

"Don't even think about scalping the fucker," Hooker told the T-Patcher. "It's against the Geneva Convention."

Just then, Flagg and Molena came back in, clutching stuff they'd salvaged from the base. Besides an armload of salami, cheese and other tasty foodstuffs, they'd brought back a mess of German guns and grenades. "There's a whole arsenal back there," Molena told the lieutenant, the bulges in his cheeks making it apparent that he'd already sampled some of the chow.

Instructing his T-Patchers to keep Von Keltrop on ice till he got back, Hooker went to check out the ordnance dump Molena and Flagg had found. Stacked to the ceiling against one wall were crates of ammo, grenades, mortar bombs and other munitions.

Also uncached by the T-Patchers were two heavy machine guns and several dozen Schmeisser submachine guns. Hooker allowed the men to grab a couple of Schmeissers for souvenirs.

Making sure there was the right equipment available to jury-rig a timed detonator, he set to work manufacturing cluster bombs out of a couple of the potato-masher grenades lashed together and placing them here and there across the room. He then called for the SS leader to be brought into the storage room.

"Take his boot off," Hooker told one of his men.

"Which boot, Lieutenant?"

"Make it the right one," Hooker replied. "Now hand me that chain."

Saying that, Hooker chained the man by his bare ankle to the iron bars covering a storm drain set in the flagstone floor.

"Fritz, we're sporting types, just like you SS guys," Hooker told the Nazi with a graveyard smile when he was finished. "So we're gonna give you a chance. This here farmhouse is gonna blow straight to kingdom come in maybe ten minutes." Saying that, he pitched his bayonet knife so that it vibrated in the wooden frame of one of the munitions crates an inch from the German's arm.

"Now, you got yourself a choice. I reckon it'll take you fifteen minutes to slice through those chains with that knife we're leaving you. Of course, you can probably cut through your ankle in only five minutes if you try hard enough."

"Nein! Nein!" shrieked the German as the Americans filed out of the room. "This is against the Geneva Convention! You cannot do such a thing. It is forbidden, I tell you—*forbidden!*"

"Nuts," Hooker said with a scowl as he set the clock timer on one of the cluster bombs positioned across the room from where the German was chained, and raced up the stairs. Von Keltrop watched the minute hand of the clock ticking away the time he had left to live and reluctantly pulled the knife from the crate. Again he stared at the moving minute hand. Then, with a cry of pain and anguish, he began sawing at his ankle until blood began to spurt....

11

Easy Company's Third Platoon was a quarter-mile away from the farmhouse when they heard the explosion. The thunder of the blast echoed off the mountainsides as the farmhouse blew sky-high.

"*Achtung,* you heinies," Private Dealey said to the two soldiers they had captured, prodding the skittish Germans ahead with the barrel of his SMG. The prisoners had stopped and reflexively turned toward the explosion when the farmhouse blew. "Keep moving or you get the same as your fancy-pants leader did."

With Hooker at the lead, the platoon wound its way down the narrow dirt road, following the same route they had come. The rain had slackened off with the coming of evening. But a heavy ground fog made the going in this rocky wilderness treacherous. Visibility was so poor that the dogfaces of Third Platoon could hardly distinguish the men in front of them from the rocks, trees and other landscape features.

Suddenly Hooker passed the word down the line for his Texans to halt. A little farther along the road, he calculated that they would be coming to the column of Panzers that they'd passed earlier on.

Hooker's mission plan had called for skirting the Panzers entirely, but in the past few minutes, he'd got to thinking. The German prisoners they had brought back from the farmhouse might have changed a thing or two in their favor. Maybe now they had themselves a shot at getting at those Panzers.

"Dealey, bring those prisoners over here on the double," Hooker ordered to his second in command.

In a couple of minutes, the two Germans stood in front of the American lieutenant.

Hooker sized both of them up. Arrogant bastards, he thought to himself. Hand-picked members of Himmler's killer SS elite. Not used to taking shit from those they considered their inferiors. But just the same, pretty shaken up right now by the way they'd got their asses kicked back there at the farmhouse.

"Either of you boys *sprechen ze* English?" Hooker asked suddenly, his gimlet eyes sweeping from face to face, alert to any change that might signal understanding. The Germans didn't register any response, though. Hooker smiled and tugged on an earlobe. "Okay," he told them, "I guess you don't."

Hooker looked over at Dealey.

"Dealey," Hooker began, staring the Nazis in the face and wearing a broad grin as he pulled a pack of Lucky Strikes from his pocket, "get behind these goose-steppers and shoot both of them through the back of the head.

"They're useless to us as prisoners, so we might as well get rid of them right now," he continued. "They don't understand a word of English, so they won't understand anything I'm saying. The kraut on the left gets it first. Shoot him when he lights up."

Still smiling, Hooker stepped in front of the leftmost prisoner and shook out a Lucky Strike from the crumpled pack. The German suddenly got a wild look in his eyes as he shoved Hooker aside and tried to jackrabbit. Dealey tackled the Hun before he got more than two feet. The SS man smashed to the ground with a wallop and a grunt, landing facedown in the sucking mud.

Unholstering his M1911 .45 automatic and cocking its hammer, Hooker hauled the man to his feet.

"This is the nitty-gritty, boy," he told the German, shoving the business end of the Colt in his bleeding face. "You're dealing with Texans now, hear? Either I hear you speak English better'n Jimmy Cagney or you get it right between the eyes."

"Do not shoot!" the wide-eyed German shrieked, his English precise but thickly accented. "I speak some English."

Hooker smiled a graveyard grin, made even more malicious looking because of three days' growth of stubble and the mud that covered his sallow-cheeked face, turning the full force of his battle stare on the Nazi.

"You got yourself a name, boy?" Hooker asked, putting away the Colt.

"I am called Gunther," came the sheepish answer. While he didn't like leaning on a beaten adversary, Hooker had to remind himself that this pathetic-looking soldier wore the death's-head patch on his sleeve. As messed up as he might be right now, Gunther was nevertheless one of Hitler's shock troops of killer elite. Showing mercy to his kind would be just plain stupid. His kind didn't even know the meaning of the word.

"Howdy, Gunther," Hooker told him with a mocking smile. "My friends call me Rudy, but you can call me Mr. Hooker."

While the prisoner took this in, Hooker continued, "Now here's what you can do for me, baby-cakes. You know them Panzers and rocket launchers you krauts got stashed a ways up the road? Well, what I want you to do is walk on over to the first one and rap your delicate little knuckles on the side. You tell the tankers you got separated from your unit and want them to open up. One of my boys'll be behind you, so don't try anything cute, unless you got your cemetery plot paid for."

Gunther agreed, nodding and saying "*Ja, ja,* I understand." Hooker instructed him to tell the other German to do the same thing.

The other prisoner shouted at Gunther in German, his eyes flashing angrily. "No! It's better to die than cooperate with American swine."

Hooker didn't need a translator to catch the drift of the words. The second man was older than Gunther, and by the looks of him, obviously a true believer in his Aryan destiny as a member of Hitler's master race. "Dealey, do the honors," Hooker said.

"With pleasure, Lieutenant," Dealey answered. Then he hauled off and knocked the second man to the ground with a well-placed haymaker to his square jaw. The German was dazed and bleeding as Dealey picked him up like a bag full of rocks.

"His jaw ain't broke," Dealey told Hooker. "Don't fret none, Lieutenant. The kraut can still talk."

"Okay, up and at 'em," Hooker said. With Gunther and the other German in the lead, Rudy's Raiders started off down the road toward the tanks.

12

San Pietro

They didn't make them any tougher than the battle-scarred doughfoots of Easy Company's Fifth Platoon. Sergeant Lou Jack Claymore had been reassigned as the platoon's NCO after his original unit, First Platoon, had suffered heavy casualties in the bloody battles to wrestle the Winter Line from German control.

Now the town of San Pietro was the next domino slated to fall to the excruciatingly slow but thankfully steady Allied advance. San Pietro clung tenaciously to the steep side of a mountain, a patch of ground critical to the success of the Allied spearhead toward Rome.

San Pietro commanded the high mountain passes leading to the Mignano Gap, a narrow defile in the craggy granite face of the towering Aurunci mountain range.

It was through this breach that the invading infantry forces would have to pass in order to achieve their objective. To fail to do so would be to invite destruction by German artillery, which could blast them off the face of the earth. Exposed and at a tactical disadvantage to the well-entrenched enemy, the infantry would be like sitting ducks.

Blood and Glory

To Lou Jack it seemed as though two things had not changed one iota since the bloody debacle at Salerno. The first thing was the cold and the rain and the mud. The second thing was that the Germans always continued to hold the high ground and all the tactical advantages that went along with it.

It wasn't any different now, he reflected from his seat in the personnel area of a big, canvas-topped ten-wheel transport truck lumbering toward the front lines outside of Rome, along with the rest of Fifth Platoon.

As Lou Jack and his T-Patchers were jostled to and fro by the juddering truck as its tires plunged into deep ruts in the muddy roadway, they could hear the incessant booming of the enormous 88 mm railway artillery guns firing in the distance. On top of all their other advantages, the Germans had succeeded in moving their heavy artillery farther and farther inland as the Allies advanced.

One thing had definitely changed, though. This was the American infantryman himself. The shavetail second-line troopers who had been flung onto the Italian beachheads had become battle-hardened fighters, easily a match for Hitler's Wehrmacht.

Suddenly a new sound became audible above the ceaseless hammering of the distant German guns. Lou Jack became alert, snapping out of his reverie as adrenaline coursed through his bloodstream.

"Hit the dirt!" he shouted as he dived over the side of the transport. "Stuka at three o'clock!"

That was all the men of Fifth Platoon needed to hear. Within seconds the distant whine of the Luftwaffe's feared JU-87 dive-bomber became a terrifying banshee screech. Sounding like the combined whine of a million giant mosquitoes, the Stuka began its notorious steep, earthward plunge at a speed of 250 miles per hour from an altitude of two hundred feet.

No dogface who had ever experienced that sound would ever be likely to forget it. The whine of the Stuka's powerful turbines punched through the human mind like an ice pick, leaving panic in its wake. The only thing that a soldier wanted to do was to escape from that sound, bury himself in the mud like a crab scuttling from some hungry bird of prey.

The JU-87's whine was feared because it was a harbinger of the release of a thousand-pound blockbuster bomb that the Stuka carried strapped beneath its wings. The plane was equipped with two such bombs, and combined with the thousands of rounds of 7.92 mm machine-gun fire the aircraft was capable of showering on unfortunate troops, the appearance of a Stuka dive-bomber meant immediate death from the air.

Lou Jack felt the earth beginning to tremble beneath him as one, then another of the blockbuster bombs plunged groundward and detonated with a thunderous explosion. Even though they struck better than a half mile away from his position, Lou Jack could feel the world shudder.

All at once the ten-wheeled transport truck suffered a direct hit from the JU-87's machine-gun fire and quickly burst into flames as its fuel lines caught fire and its gas tank exploded. Then, as quickly as it had appeared, the Stuka's banshee scream diminished to a small, far-off whine again as it flew off again, probably to refuel and replenish its ammo supply.

"On your feet, you sorry assholes!" Lou Jack shouted out to his T-Patchers after checking for casualties. There were two dead and two wounded. Both of the latter had been hit by ricochets. They would be turned over to the care of the medics, who now raced up in field ambulances marked with red crosses.

"Move out fast! It's only a matter of time before kraut artillery drops a couple of big ones on our position to finish the job," Lou Jack went on, his voice booming out its warning.

As the T-Patchers set off down the road, grumbling among themselves, they could see the injured men carted away on pea green canvas stretchers into field ambulances that had quickly pulled up in the aftermath of the Stuka attack on the American infantry column heading toward Rome. The line of burning vehicles and wounded littering both ends of the roadside testified to the deadly accuracy of the Stukas and the military precision of their pilots.

Lou Jack reflected that death was death, and while the men who'd been hit were no luckier than the doughfoots who'd bought it on the beachheads of Salerno and Anzio, in some ways they were better off. There had been no ambulances on the beachheads, after all. Most of the time not even morphine had been available. Worse than that, there had been no place to go with the wounded—the invading infantry had been hopelessly pinned down.

Lighting the cigar that had gone out during the commotion of the Stuka attack, Lou Jack hitched his field pack higher on his broad shoulders and loped off to join the column of his advancing platoon.

THE GERMANS HAD DUG IN deep and were fighting to maintain their hold on the town of San Pietro with everything they had and for as long as they were able. Along with the rest of the infantry, the T-Patchers found themselves up against elements of the Sixteenth Panzer Division and SS troops of the elite Adolf Hitler Liebstandarte, some of the Nazi fatherland's toughest troops.

Both the special Waffen SS and the regular Wehrmacht combat units were fighters to be reckoned with. They were men to be feared and respected on the battlefield.

The Germans were watching when the infantry entered the town from the south. Dug in within the remains of buildings that had been carpet bombed to rubble, they opened up with withering firepower.

Most of the town had been destroyed by the Germans themselves as part of a defensive strategy. Ruined buildings made for much better protective cover than intact ones. There were far more sheltered areas to attack from and retreat to. Men, fighting a dirty battle, had finally learned to obey the logic of cornered rats.

Fifth Platoon came loping into the combat zone just behind the Grant tank that they had caught up with on the outskirts of the city. The tankers agreed to give them cover as they entered the German-held sector of San Pietro and shell the enemy positions before the infantry troops moved in.

While the T-Patchers crouched behind the tank, the Grant's howitzer pivoted back and forth, lobbing magnesium cluster bombs into the already saturation-bombed rubble of the Italian ghost town.

The effect of the Grant's incendiary barrage was total and immediate demolition. Each shell exploded in a miniature firestorm, creating sudden infernos where ammo stores or gas lines ignited and sent clouds of pulverized rubble spewing many feet into the air.

Continuing to lay down a carpet of fire to soften up the enemy's defenses, the Grant clanked ponderously forward, the mine-sweeper fittings on its glacis detonating—and thereby neutralizing—the high-explosive Teller mines that had been sewn along the access route into the territory the enemy controlled.

When the Grant had completed its grim work, dazing and stunning the enemy by smashing and blasting their fortified positions to pulverized ruins, Lou Jack's T-Patchers raced headlong into the swirling haze of battle smoke. Swallowed by the stinking death clouds and inhaling the choking vapors of exploding ordnance, the T-Patchers marched forward into the open mouth of hell.

13

Rounding the corner of the square, the German patrol car suddenly materialized with no advance warning. The open-topped car was outfitted with a .50-caliber pintle-mounted machine gun and bore the Nazi swastika emblazoned on its flanks. For a few seconds the Germans looked as surprised as the American dogfaces were, facing each other across a small cobblestone piazza that formed the apex of two narrow, alleylike streets.

Having turned to come abreast of a building at the end of a narrow cobbled street that might have been called picturesque before war savagely altered its appearance, the squad of Fifth Platoon T-Patchers had walked headlong into the enemy who were halted in the piazza.

Reacting a second too slowly for his own good, Private Ray McAllister was stitched across the chest as he prepared to lob the grenade he'd yanked from shoulder webbing. Clattering to the cobbled paving stones, the grenade rolled a couple of inches, then went off with a loud bang, blowing McAllister to smithereens and killing the fellow standing nearest to him in the process.

While this was happening, Lou Jack was hunkered behind the protection of the iron wellhead in the piazza's center, a rifle grenade fitted into the barrel of his

M-1. A trigger squeeze, and the 40 mm mortar round was launched from the M-1's muzzle with a wallop that reverberated off the stone buildings on either side of the piazza. It sailed through the air on a flat trajectory toward the Nazi position.

The grenade round detonated with an earsplitting report just short of the patrol car. Proximity-fused, it exploded as an airburst that flung shrapnel across a twenty-foot blast radius. Razor-edged fragments scythed through the SS officer who was standing up in the staff car, fisting a wickedly gleaming blued-steel P-38 that he waved about as he barked orders at his troops.

Hit in midsentence, the officer clutched the bloody remnants of his sheared-away face and flopped head-first over the side of the open-topped vehicle, his knees on the staff car's running board and his gleaming black boots hooked over the edge of the passenger side door.

"Spread out! Keep your heads *down!*" Lou Jack shouted out as the final echoes of the explosion died away. Having thrown their dead leader out of the car, the goose-steppers were already scattering for cover.

The squad of camouflage-fatigued SS commandos broke and dodged to concealed positions in doorways and flattened behind the cover of wrecked vehicles. The distinctive camos—or *tarnjacken*—marked this bunch as members of the elite Deutschland Regiment, deployed in mountain fighting. In the narrow street that meandered through the mountain town, it was difficult for either side to maneuver with any effectiveness, and so neither enjoyed a clear-cut advantage.

From the German positions, bursts of autofire twinkled from the Schmeisser SMGs, but the firing ceased abruptly when the Nazis, like the Americans, sensed a stalemate in the wind. In the temporary lull, punctuated by the crackle of the burning staff car, Lou Jack began to formulate a plan.

"Hutchins and Lennox! Front and center on the double!" he called out, then outlined his plan. "Get up onto the roofs of those buildings and circle behind them Germans. As soon as you're in position, let 'em have it with these hand grenades."

Clutching their weapons, the men sprinted off, the grenades carried in musette bags at their waists. Lou Jack smiled grimly. The raw shavetails who had stormed the beachheads at Salerno had been rapidly tempered like drop-forged steel by the rigors of war. By the violent alchemy of combat, they had been transformed into blooded fighters in the combat crucible of total war.

Those dogfaces who had survived, that is. The unlucky son of a bitches who hadn't already paid the heavy price for being sent out with more guts than hard combat training to take on some of the most veteran troops in Hitler's army.

But it wasn't the time to get bogged down with philosophizing, Lou Jack knew. Nor was he really inclined to do so. That crap could wait until the shooting stopped. Shouting and resorting to sign language when his shouts were drowned out by the din of a fresh volley of autofire from the German positions, Lou Jack ordered his T-Patchers to keep the adversary covered.

As he took off, though, Lennox stumbled and fell, hit by a 9 mm fusillade of Schmeisser lead.

"Damn!" Lou Jack cursed, watching Lennox hit the cobblestones on his face, roll once, then lie faceup with arms and legs outflung in death. He wouldn't ask for any more volunteers, the sergeant decided. Seeing that Hutchins had successfully gained the entrance of a house about thirty yards to his left, Lou Jack took off on his own, the stink of cordite fresh in his nostrils.

A hailstorm of parabellums kicked up a line of sparks on the cobbled street at his running heels. Inches ahead of the bursts of flying Krupp steel, the Texan succeeded in reaching the relative safety of the house just as a 40 mm *grenatwerfer* round tore a chunk out of the plaster doorway inches from his head with a clap like mountain thunder.

Hugging the peeling plaster wall and keeping his Tommy gun ready for the few seconds it took his eyes to adjust to the relative darkness of the building's interior, Lou Jack listened to the sound of the firefight outside. The staccato music of automatic fire was punctuated by the guttural screams of the enemy and the curses of his own embattled men and the occasional thud of a grenade round detonating.

He swallowed hard, feeling his heart jackhammer in his chest, and wiped sweat from his forehead with the back of his dirty sleeve, inhaling the sour odor of the building mixed with the smells of cordite smoke and high explosive wafting in from the street.

Lou Jack jumped and raised the Thompson when something ran through a beam of sunlight shining down from the skylight five stories up. The black cat rubbed up against his legs, purring as if Lou Jack were a long-lost friend. The Texan told the cat to scat, suddenly superstitious—the black cat had crossed his path. Then he ran for the staircase and picked his way carefully up the flight of creaking wooden stairs.

As he ascended, he made sure to keep his profile low in case any hitters were waiting for him on one of the shadowed upper landings above. A moment later he was glad that he had taken care to be diligent.

Waiting for Lou Jack on the upper landing was a German. Standing at the next landing in front of an open doorway, he clutched a Schmeisser SMG. In the split-instant view, Lou Jack saw a bullet-shaped head, a puckered, half-moon scar going down one side of the face and a heavy, compact body.

Knowing that the Nazi hardman was about to let him have it, Lou Jack vaulted the banister, one step ahead of the line of parabellum rivets spat out by the rotoring, full-auto SMG.

Rising quickly to one knee, the dogface returned Thompson SMG fire from the hip, seeing the ambusher duck into the doorway a heartbeat in front of the glowing lance of .45-caliber man-shredders that chewed into plaster and lath instead of human flesh.

Snapping a fresh clip of heavy-caliber rounds into the Tommy's receiver, Lou Jack hotfooted it up the flight of stairs toward the room above, his burp gun poised at the ready in case the bushwhacker got himself a notion to make like a jack-in-the-box and jump out, spitting fire and lead. Diving low as he reached the room, Lou Jack calculated that the line of Schmeisser

Blood and Glory

fire would come several inches higher as he popped up with the Tommy gun in death-deal position.

The German hadn't taken the T-Patcher's gambit, however. This hitter was nobody's fool. He was waiting for the American with his lethal black machine pistol clutched tightly in his big fists, aimed directly at his heart.

"Drop your weapon," the big, scowling Nazi demanded in a voice thick with contempt.

In one brawny arm the German gripped the throat of a half-naked Italian woman whose large brown eyes were wet with terror.

Lou Jack harbored no illusions about what would happen if he let go of the Tommy gun. Scar Face would have no qualms about blowing him straight to hell and shoving the woman against the wall before taking it on the arches.

"Nuts to you," Lou Jack snarled.

The German's scowl turned even blacker. Lou Jack figured scowling lessons must have been a part of his basic training, because the guy had it down to an art form.

"Stay back," the Hun barked in bad English, jerking the barrel of his Schmeisser to the left to indicate that Lou Jack was to step in that direction as he advanced toward the center of the room.

Suddenly pulling a surprise move, though, the girl kicked him in the shins and half jumped, half fell to the floor. Lou Jack's Tommy gun chattered raucously a pulse-beat later. The Schmeisser coughed once, but the shot was wild and went awry, striking Lou Jack in the fleshy part of his left arm. But the German wasn't as fortunate as his opponent. Catapulted backward by a volley of .45-caliber steel, he crashed through the wooden balustrade and plunged four stories straight down.

Checking his wound, Lou Jack was relieved to find that the fat parabellum slug had passed clean through his arm. Good thing the krauts didn't use rimfire cartridges, he thought to himself, knowing his luck was still holding good.

The girl lay sobbing in a corner, but Lou Jack had no time to console her. He had other things on his mind just then.

Leaving the *putana* where she was, he hustled up to the top floor of the building, this time encountering no opposition, but painfully aware of the ratcheting of automatic gunfire coming from the piazza below. Shimmying fast up a ladder, the sergeant pushed through and stuck his helmeted head into empty space.

Crawling across the rooftop on his belly, Lou Jack peered over the edge of the red clay roof tiles. The SS shooters deployed on either side of the burning staff car were still engaged in a firefight with his unit. Peering over at the rooftop of the building across the narrow street, he could see that Hutchins was already in position. Lou Jack flashed the T-Patcher the thumbs-up as he pulled his grenades from shoulder webbing, popped the pins and sent the Mills fraggers tumbling downward to do their grisly work in the piazza below like ripe black fruits dropping from the tree of death.

Ku-thuk! Kuhhhh-thukkkk!

The two grenades went off almost simultaneously, scoring perfect bull's-eyes on German flesh and bone.

Lou Jack saw one man go flying through the air as though he'd been catapulted from some unseen trampoline to land in a motionless, broken heap on the bloodstained cobbles. The rest of the platoon took advantage of the surprise attack to make a frontal assault on the other enemy positions and clean out the remaining Nazis in a hail of fire, leaving none of them alive to *Sieg* and *Heil* anymore.

Hustling streetside again, Lou Jack wondered what the hell the Germans had been doing in front of the door of the building at which the staff car had been pulling up when they'd encountered them. The special uniforms they'd been wearing were also a puzzle. The door wasn't marked with any kind of sign to indicate what lay beyond, but most of the buildings in these parts didn't look like anything special from the outside.

Lou Jack was surprised when the door to the building fronting the piazza suddenly opened. An old man in a priest's black cassock held it open and smiled at him.

"*Prego, prego.* Come in, come in," he told Lou Jack, his face beaming, beckoning as he spoke. "We have been expecting you."

As if that in itself had not been a shock, Lou Jack's jaw hung gaping as he saw what was behind the old priest. The rest of his men stared goggle-eyed and slack jawed, too. Now the T-Patcher NCO had a pretty good notion of what the Nazis had been protecting.

14

There were at least a dozen streetwalkers gathered in the parlor of the villa off the small piazza. Lou Jack knew they were hookers because if they weren't, then he'd been spending his time in all the wrong places. The girls eyed Lou Jack's dogfaces from top to bottom. The men of Fifth Platoon unabashedly returned the appraising stares and licked their lips.

"What the hell's going on here, Padre?" Lou Jack asked after he'd ascertained that the priest spoke English. To say the least, the friar didn't look like the kind of a guy who'd be running a house of ill repute. No matter which way he looked at the situation, things just didn't add up right.

"Che cosa molta, molta brutta," the friar said in answer to the American's question, spreading his hands in a gesture of helplessness. "I am afraid that this war has turned the world upside down. Yet these women, too, are the Lord's children."

"Yeah, well the krauts ain't one or the other, that's for sure," Lou Jack replied, half-smoked cigar stuck in the corner of his mouth. "You know anything about why those SS guys we ran into outside were so interested in this place, Padre?"

"Perhaps, yes," the little friar told him, his brown eyes flashing the Texan a look of profound sadness. "But first have a drink with me." He produced an unlabeled bottle of red wine and uncorked it with his teeth. "It is a long story, and not one fit for telling with a parched throat," he said as he poured, no longer looking quite as sad.

IT WAS AN ABOMINATION! Corporal Thurmond Love, called Preacher Man by the troops, could not describe it any other way. This was not a house of God, surely. Yet nevertheless he didn't think the women were to be treated as objects of lust and licentiousness.

"Why you no like me touch you there?" the whore called LaDonna asked, wearing Preacher Man's helmet, her blouse hanging open to reveal two firm, round breasts. "You no like girls?"

Preacher Man pushed LaDonna's probing hand away. The rest of the Texans watching in the room guffawed as they looked on.

"He don't even like the good parts, do you, Preacher Man?" one of the T-Patchers asked as Preacher Man stormed out of the room, pulling up his unzipped fly. "Hey, y'all come over here, little lady," the same GI called out to the one who'd taunted Preacher Man. "Game's not over yet."

A half-dozen members of Fifth Platoon were arranged around a large circular oak table in the cathouse's basement. There was a card deck at the center of the table.

Streetwalkers in various stages of undress were seated at the table, some atop the laps of GIs. All were drunk on grappa, which the girls swigged straight from the bottle but the Americans drank GI-style, cut with reconstituted orange juice from their K-rations.

"This is really how Americans play poker, yes?" asked Teressina, who came over and took a seat on Hutchins's lap. She stuck her ample bosom in his face.

"Damn sure is, honey."

As the game continued, the girls had on less and less clothes and more and more of themselves sticking out. Private Wayne Hutchins and Teressina soon found themselves alone in another section of the basement.

Teressina giggled and squirmed closer to Hutchins. She quickly freed him and began ministering to him, cooing playfully as he sucked in his breath in pleased surprise.

Touching her hair, Hutchins pretended that it was his girlfriend, Mary-Ellen, back home in Austin who was doing those things to him, even though Mary-Ellen had never done anything quite like this. When he got back Stateside, he decided then and there, maybe they would have to try some new things.

Moments later Hutchins threw back his head and groaned loudly, and Teressina laughed with pleasure at the boy who had been so easy to please and told him that what had just taken place was merely for openers.

"Where's the can, honey?" Hutchins asked a little while later, suddenly having other things on his mind. "All that wine, you *capisc'?*"

"Si, capito," she answered him with a laugh. "Around corner, you go there, okay?" Hutchins left Teressina, who was already beginning to party without him. What a babe, he thought. Them Italian dames sure were hot, and that was no bullshit.

Having got the picture that he was to relieve himself on the floor anywhere convenient, Hutchins stumbled through the darkness to the far end of the cellar. The cellar had been constructed in the days of the Roman Caesars, like most of the foundations of the ancient hill town. The walls stank oppressively of dank, moldering stone, and centuries of dripping water had festooned the ceiling with stalactites three feet long.

Having done his duty, Hutchins tried to find his way back to Teressina in the darkness. But the darkness and his drunkenness caused him to stumble and fall.

"Aw, Jesus!" Hutchins cried out, and heard the fruity snap of rotten planking as he plunged downward precipitously. Fortunately for the dogface, the fall wasn't all that steep. Shaking his head as he picked himself up from the slimy stone surface, Hutchins groped in his pocket and struck a match. For the second time since entering the cathouse, Hutchins's jaw gaped in open disbelief. He just plain could not believe his eyes.

PREACHER MAN CAME upon Lou Jack and the old friar in a righteous huff. "Sergeant, I have to report misconduct on the part of the men. They are—" he groped for words "—I guess you'd call it *fraternizing* with the women."

"You mean they're dipping their old wazoos in some local poon-tang? That what you mean, boy?" Lou Jack replied with a laugh.

Preacher Man stood there with an expression on his face that made him look for all the world as if he'd just been blackjacked. The old friar began guffawing every bit as hard as Lou Jack was.

"My son, these men do not sin," Friar Paolo said when he was in control of himself again. "The women give themselves willingly. Have some wine." He poured out the dregs of the bottle and held out a glass to the T-Patcher. Muttering something about blasphemy, Preacher Man stormed out of the room, leaving the wine untouched, and being unceremoniously elbowed aside by Hutchins, who was on his way in.

"Hey, Sarge," Hutchins shouted excitedly, waving his arms. "You ain't never gonna believe what I found down there. It's—"

"I know all about it," Lou Jack told him without batting an eye. "The good Father Paolo here's been telling me the whole crazy story."

"That is correct, my son," Friar Paolo put in, punctuating his sentence with a winy belch. "It was revealed to me in a vision that you brave soldiers would be coming to me. When I heard the knock at the door, the girls, they were afraid. They thought that it was the Germans coming back to get them. I, however, knew better. I knew that our blessed salvation had finally arrived."

"I don't get it, Sarge," Hutchins said, scratching his crew-cut head with puzzlement.

"Don't worry," Lou Jack told him. "You will."

15

For the moment the monastery was behind German lines, commanding the approach to the Liri Valley, and beyond that, the Allied strategic objective of Rome itself. The ancient structure stood atop the towering massif of Monte Cassino.

For well over a month, as the incessant boom of U.S. artillery batteries drew ever closer, elements of SS Division Hermann Goering had been methodically ransacking the monastery's priceless art collection. Treasures amassed over the course of three centuries were being plundered in the space of weeks.

In spite of their actions, the Nazis had been reaping huge propaganda bonuses. In addition to the plunder, the Goebbels propaganda machine was portraying their efforts to strip the monastery of its paintings, tapestries, sculptures and other priceless artifacts in the newsreels and the papers as an effort on behalf of culture and civilization to save them from Allied bombs.

Reichsmarshal Hermann Goering, chief of the Gestapo and a fanatic art collector, was skimming the most valuable artifacts for his own private collection at Karinhall, his hunting lodge forty-five miles southeast of Berlin. There, the new plunder from Cassino would join untold other artworks looted from every town and city that the greedy hand of the German Reich could reach.

But the Nazis had not got hold of all the booty at Cassino. The most precious relics—statuettes of silver and gold containing the remains of the patron saints of the abbey at Monte Cassino—had been spirited away well before the methodical plunder of the SS had commenced.

The path of the artifacts—in themselves representing a treasure of incalculable worth—had led to a smaller monastery several miles away near the town of Venafro. The arrival of SS plunder details attached to Goering's Bureau of Reich Culture, however, necessitated another hasty move before the relics were captured by the advancing Germans.

Eventually the relics found a resting place in a convent near San Pietro. But the convent was severely damaged by an artillery shell lobbed by British artillery guns in the direction of Cassino. They were then removed to the most unlikely place, imaginable only by a quirk of fate.

That came about when one of the girls of Mama Caterina's House of the Purple Veronica was taken in by a nun after having been raped by a group of SS men. The girl had overheard the sisters of the convent discussing the Cassino relics and offered to hide them at her place of employment. After recovering from their initial shock, the nuns too saw no other choice. Friar Paolo, attached to the convent, came along with the relics to insure they were properly handled.

The nuns who remained behind at the convent were not as fortunate as the relics that they had sent to safety. Before they had the opportunity to escape, the Germans marched in. The SS raped—and then tortured and killed—all the nuns in the convent. The relics were never found. Alone among them, only Friar Paolo had escaped with his life.

Lou Jack took a deep drag on his cigar as he finished giving his assembled T-Patchers the rundown on the situation.

"That's it in a nutshell," he told them by way of conclusion. "What the padre wants is for us to move the relics out of this here cathouse and over to the other church where they'll be safe."

"Ain't that a matter for G-2 or something?" Private Hutchins wanted to know.

"I don't know, Sarge," another dogface put in, "this whole deal sounds like it might be a court-martialable offense."

"The way I look at it," Lou Jack broke in, "we're answerable to nobody besides our own consciences here. But what it all boils down to is just one thing— how many are in and how many are out. Let's see a show of hands."

All the hands went up except Preacher Man's. "This is blasphemy! Sheer blasphemy!" he shouted.

"I guess that means we're going, except for Preacher Man, who the girls can baby-sit till we get back," Lou Jack said with a wink to the padre, who thanked the men of Fifth Platoon. "There's only one minor problem you ought to know about, boys," he went on. "The place we're going to... Technically speaking, it's still behind German lines."

AFTER THE INITIAL excitement had worn off, Lou Jack realized that there was no way in hell that Fifth Platoon was about to pull this detail off without the assistance of Easy Company's commander, Captain Murch Cody.

With Cody's help they might just be able to promote the required transport and avoid being chucked in the company guardhouse as a bunch of AWOL goldbricks. Or worse—their little foray behind German lines might be misconstrued by some as being outright treason.

So it was that Lou Jack bid so-long to one of Mama Caterina's lovely signorinas and went off in search of Captain Cody.

"You gotta be outa your cotton pickin' mind, Sergeant!" Cody had blustered. "No way in the world can I be a party to this kind of horseshit. *No* fucking way!"

Lou Jack had been careful to omit any mention of the prostitutes, and was glad he had done so. With the girls involved, the captain's strong puritanical streak would have certainly induced him to eight-ball the idea as soon as spit at it.

After a while, though, Cody's natural Texan orneriness got the better of him, and he gave in to Lou Jack's request. Hell, Cody figured. What were they all fighting for, anyway? This mission was certainly in the line of duty—depending on how you looked at it, that is.

Lou Jack could tell that Cody was really getting into the idea when the captain unlocked a footlocker and brought out a bunch of oilskin carrying pouches. Inside were a couple of stubby black cylinders.

"Got no idea what these are, Sergeant?"

Lou Jack shook his head. He'd never seen anything like them before.

"These here are what you call sound suppressors," Cody explained, holding one out. "They fit the threading of the M-3 submachine guns with which I know you're familiar. You screw in one of these babies, and your fire will make less noise than a sneeze. Hijacked 'em from the OSS boys," he concluded with pride.

Since they were going out on a night mission, the silencers might come in handy if they happened to run into any enemy patrols, Cody explained.

THE CATACOMBS MEANDERED beneath the ancient town, while overhead scudding clouds concealed a waning moon. The catacombs terminated on the outskirts of the town, not more than a few score feet from the British motor pool. Dog-robbing a truck away from the Brits appealed to the Texans, to whom the English were an alien breed.

It wasn't so much that the T-Patchers didn't admire their courage or considered them inferior fighting men—just the opposite, in fact. Anybody who could singlehandedly hold off Hitler's Luftwaffe the way the Brits had been doing for years was plainly worthy of a Texan's admiration and respect. It was just that the British soldier with his spit-and-polish and snappy salutes acted in a manner that was the direct opposite of the way Texans thought and acted. Swiping transport appealed to the larcenous streak in all the T-Patchers.

"I say, Captain," the British lieutenant in command of the motor pool exclaimed to Cody as he studied the requisition orders Cody had quickly typed up after a hasty side trip to headquarters, a mixture of

Texas double-talk and official-looking seals. "This is most irregular. You state that you've been ordered to take two of our vehicles out on a cloak-and-dagger mission of some sort."

The Brit looked up from the requisition forms and gave Cody and Lou Jack the once-over. From the puzzled expression on his face, it was obvious he didn't believe they were secret-mission material.

He looked back down at the orders Cody had handed him and made a show of studying them. "Why not requisition American vehicles? I still fail to understand it."

"Like I told you, Major," Cody drawled to the Englishman, "these here orders come right down from the top."

"Mmm, quite," the Brit returned absently, again looking at the forms. "By the way, I hold the rank of lieutenant," he added, though Cody could tell he'd been impressed by having been called "major." "Perhaps a chat with your commanding officer might be in order." The Brit reached for the phone on a low trestle table nearby. "What did you say your name was?"

"I didn't," Cody told the lieutenant. "Look, I got orders not to talk to anybody about this, but you leave me no choice. What I'm about to tell you is in strictest confidence. Do you read me, Major?"

The Brit nodded, this time not bothering to correct Cody as to his rank.

"Okay, it's like this," Cody began. "You heard of the OSS, right? Well, while we're wasting time dorking around here, a top British agent is being smuggled back behind enemy lines. Now, you got any idea who this OSS guy's been sent into Germany to gather Intelligence on?" Cody went on. "I can't say his name, but if you look at my partner here, you might be able to figure out who I mean."

Lou Jack held his forefingers under his nose. Clicking his heels, he stuck his left arm straight out, palm up in a Nazi *Sieg Heil*. The Brit swallowed hard. A few minutes later Murch Cody and Lou Jack Claymore were tooling out of the motor pool in a ten-wheeled transport vehicle.

"How long do you figure before he realizes we just sold him a line of bullshit longer than the Mississippi?" Lou Jack asked the captain.

"Just hope it's long enough for us to do what we're out to do," Cody said just as the big truck's headlight beams picked out the forms of their fellow travelers on the midnight mercy run.

16

The transport carrying Easy Company's Fifth Platoon and Friar Paolo Provenzano negotiated the hairpin twists and turns of a mountain road that was switchbacked more sharply than the creases on a bird colonel's parade uniform.

The men had said their goodbyes to the girls at Mama Caterina's House of the Purple Veronica and were eager to get the job of stashing the precious relics over and done with so they could hustle back to their own lines.

Only a little while before, each of the doggies had felt a little bit like knights of old riding off to do battle for their ladies fair. Now, though, as the truck trundled down the road away from friendly territory, the T-Patchers all began to wonder whether or not they hadn't been snookered into putting their gonads on the chopping block for something that they'd all likely live to regret.

Not that it mattered a darn anymore. It was too late to turn back. Besides, when a Texan gave his word, it was a promise sealed in concrete.

Since the friar knew the way, he sat up front beside the driver, Private Bobby "Hot Rod" Hillihann, a former stock-car racer on the Houston-to-Phoenix demolition derby circuit. Lou Jack and Captain Cody sat at the left and right of the cab and directly behind it in the canvas-topped stake-side rear of the British transport.

From their positions behind the cab they could converse with Hillihann and the friar both, while keeping a weather eye trained on the surrounding terrain. Both Lou Jack and the captain were as nervous as bridegrooms. These hills belonged to the *Sieg Heil*ers. Their combat senses were making them all feel mighty jumpy.

All of a sudden Hot Rod yanked the transport rig to a sudden halt. Lou Jack and Cody could immediately see why he'd done what he had. As the truck climbed the road that followed the ridge line, they could discern a large structure looming up in the near distance.

From the appearance of the place, it was some kind of medieval château or castle, now partially in ruins. But a glorious example of the local architecture wasn't what had attracted their attention. It was the swastika flag that fluttered high above the ancient battlements.

"Padre, what the hell is *that?*" Cody asked Friar Provenzano. The old priest turned in his seat and craned his neck to better see the building.

"This development is new to me," he said to Cody with a shrug of his frail shoulders. "When I first took my leave of the abbey that is to be our destination, the ruins of this castle were uninhabited. The Nazis must have taken the place over only within the past few weeks."

That analysis made sense, all right. But from the looks of the castle, it housed at least a brigade of Wehrmacht troops.

"What's your impression, Cody?" Lou Jack asked the captain in the informal manner T-Patchers felt free to use with one another, regardless of rank. "We scrub this one or what?"

"Hell's bells," Cody returned, rubbing his stubbled chin and chewing the stub of his cigar. "I suppose if them krauts are sound sleepers and if this here monastery we're bringing the goods to is as close as the padre says it is, then we might as well get this here milk run over with."

Lou Jack told Hillihann to put the transport in gear and to keep his eyeballs peeled for the Hun. To the rest of the men of the platoon, he passed the order to look sharp and sing out in case they eyeballed anything that looked important, but not to fire unless he gave the order. Settling down to wait, the troops watched the swastika banner fluttering above the castle disappear on their left as the truck rolled on into the darkness of the wooded hills.

THE T-PATCHERS ARRIVED at the monastery of San Rocco Maggiore after negotiating another two miles or so of torturous mountain road. The monastery was in a partially ruined state—as with most of the buildings dotting the wooded slopes, it had been the innocent victim of stray artillery rounds fired by both the German and American sides.

A stone outbuilding whose roof had caved in looked like a good place to stash the transport. Hillihann tucked the truck away behind a section of bomb-mangled wall that would provide it with excellent camouflage against spotter planes and patrols. Friar Provenzano told the GIs to wait a few moments while he went and roused the abbot from his slumbers. A few minutes later, the friar reappeared, accompanied by the abbot.

The two priests made quite a study in contrasts. Whereas Friar Paolo was slender of frame and stoop shouldered with a bald head and a small, well-tended goatee, Abbot Angelo was stout, round in the belly and sported an unkempt mane of shaggy gray hair.

"Come in, come in, my friends," the portly abbot greeted the American GIs, obviously overjoyed to see them and gesturing elaborately as only Italians knew how. "I see that our prayers have been answered. This is truly a great benediction that you have brought tonight."

"Where do you want us to put the goods, Padre?" Cody asked Abbot Angelo. The abbot told him to place the crates containing the Cassino relics just inside the confines of the abbey.

The two lay brothers who shared the abbey with the abbot would see to placing the crates in the abbey's basement for safekeeping. As a squad of T-Patchers offloaded the crates containing the relics, the rest of the dogfaces and the two commanders joined the priests inside the rectory.

Again locally fermented wine was brought out and glasses of the full-bodied vino poured. Unlike the case with other monastic orders, the one to which the friars belonged had tended vineyards since their founder's time hundreds of years ago. Before the war their bottled vintage had in itself paid for the upkeep of the monastery.

"Now our fields lie fallow, and most of the brothers have left this place forever," Abbot Angelo lamented as he tossed back a glass of wine and quickly poured himself another. "However, with your arrival and that of the relics, I pray that our travails will soon come to an end."

"I'll drink to that," Cody said as he hoisted his own wineglass and downed the tart contents. "Well, Padre, we've gotta be moving on," he said as he stood up not too long after, shouldering his SMG. "Glad to be of service."

Angelo's smiling demeanor changed suddenly as Cody stood to go. He traded glances with Friar Provenzano. The two priests then exchanged a few words in their native Italian.

"Scusi, signore," Abbot Angelo told Cody after the brief conversation was over, "but I think you should remain here a little while longer. I fear that there is something else you should know about."

17

Captain Murch Cody was thunderstruck by what Abbot Angelo had just revealed to him. If what the portly man told him was true, then he was sitting on Intelligence that could potentially shorten the war in Italy by months and save thousands of lives in the process.

Cody had little doubt that the abbot was not handing him a line of bull. The letter he held in his pudgy hand spelled everything out, chapter and verse. The letter bore the seal of the abbot of the great monastery that sat atop the high massif of Monte Cassino.

It was as obvious to Murch Cody as it was to Allied Commander in Chief Dwight Eisenhower that Cassino held the key to the taking of Nazi-dominated Rome. The towering massif of Cassino stood strategically at the apex of the Liri Valley, formed by the junction of the Aurunci and Abruzzi mountain ranges.

Situated at the juncture of these great mountain chains, Cassino straddled Highway 6—the road to Rome that American, British, Polish and Free French forces were taking back from the Germans inch by bloody inch.

Even as Cody sat there with Lou Jack and the friar and the abbot, Eisenhower and his opposite number on the British side, General Montgomery, were racking their brains over the question of how to deal with Cassino.

The ancient monastery nestled at the mountain's peak was the center of the controversy. Troops fighting and dying on the rocky slaughter ground of the mountain highlands surrounding Cassino had all sworn the same thing. German artillery spotters deployed within the confines of Cassino were calling down accurate fire on them, they claimed, against which they had little chance of defense or survival.

The issue was further complicated by the fact that there was no conclusive evidence one way or the other to either confirm or deny the existence of hidden German artillery spotters at Cassino monastery.

To break the deadlock, Eisenhower had sent in his right-hand man, the "glamour-boy" general, Mark Clark, whose own Intelligence report stated conclusively there were as much as a battalion of Germans holed up at Cassino.

But the letter that Cody held in his hands flew in the face of these claims and counterclaims. Bearing the official wax seal of the ancient Benedictine order to which the monastery's friars belonged, it stated beyond any shadow of a doubt that no German troops were sequestered within the monastery. The letter went on to plead for Allied forces to spare the ancient cloister from destruction.

"I myself have been to the monastery," Friar Paolo told Cody while Abbot Angelo nodded in agreement, a goblet of wine in his hand. "There are many routes in and out of the place. The Germans do not hold every one of them, nor can they possibly know of but a few of them."

"If you know all this," Lou Jack asked the old priest, "then why the heck didn't you tell us back there in San Pietro?"

"Abbot Angelo had the letter from the abbot at Cassino," the friar answered, tapping the sheet of paper that Cody clutched in his hands. "Without it and Abbot Angelo's testimony, I feared that my story would be dismissed out of hand as the ravings of a lunatic."

"Damn," was all Cody said, shaking his head, then "damn" again. There was no time to sit around debating the whys and wherefores, because this Intelligence was nothing less than dynamite. Cody had to bring it to the attention of his own commanding officer, Major General Hoagland, as soon as possible.

A thought that brightened things somewhat for Cody was that once Hoagland got a load of this new Intelligence for himself, he'd be too fired up to question very closely where it had come from.

That might solve the problem of having to explain the theft of the British transport and a platoon of AWOL American dogfaces, among other things.

"How about you, Padre?" Cody asked Friar Paolo, tucking the abbot of Cassino's letter away in the pocket of his field jacket. "Will you be coming back to San Pietro with us?"

"No, my son," the friar returned with a shake of his head and a sigh. "I will stay here with Father Angelo for a time. Together we will pray that the Germans soon leave these mountains forever."

"All right, Sergeant," Cody told Lou Jack. "Tell the boys to saddle up. We've got some hard riding ahead of us."

THE COMMANDEERED British transport lurched its way down the winding road toward the mountain town of San Pietro. Lighter by several hundred-odd pounds since its trip toward the abbey, the heavy rig rode more smoothly on the badly rutted roads.

But the loss of extra weight gave the vehicle less traction on the turns. Hot Rod Hillihann had to manhandle the wheel, ball the clutch and pump the brakes to negotiate the sharply switchbacking turns in the road without plunging toward destruction in the defiles that yawned precipitously below. Driving without headlights in the dead of night, it was no small feat.

In the inky darkness none of the passengers aboard the lumbering transport even noticed the appearance of the mechanized German column until they were practically right on top of the German unit.

"Krauts dead ahead!" Lou Jack exclaimed in a low growl, taking care not to let his voice carry over the rumble and whine of the hard-laboring Wehrmacht vehicles as they struggled to climb uphill. The rest of the platoon added choice comments of their own while unshipping their weapons.

"Cripes, Sarge. What do I do?" asked Hot Rod from behind the transport's wheel as he shifted into low gear.

"Don't do a damn thing," Lou Jack instructed the wheelman, keeping his eyes glued to the German column, studying the faces of the helmeted passengers in the cab of the lead vehicle. "Just pull over to the left side of the road, keep right on rolling and keep your fingers crossed."

Doing exactly as Lou Jack had told him, Hot Rod swung the heavy transport over to the side of the narrow road, cursing as the rig's big front tires almost slithered into a wide ditch.

The column passed abreast of the truck and kept right on going. First a staff car, then two more half-track troop carriers and finally a half-track with an antiaircraft gun mounted on top of it, slogged past up the steeply graded hill.

Few of the Germans in the column so much as glanced the T-Patchers' way. Those who did bother to take notice of the truck that passed them on the road didn't seem to question its presence or pay more than a moment's attention to it.

In the pitch darkness of the tree-canopied road, with its headlights damped and its insignia bespattered with dried road mud, the transport and its contingent of dogfaces didn't look much different from their German counterparts who were heading off in the other direction.

Once having left the German column behind them, Hot Rod in the commandeered transport kept negotiating the treacherous turns for another few miles before all on board the truck heard a sudden ominous sound. It was the cough and sputter of a dying engine.

Hot Rod hopped out of the cab and tried to get the engine going again, but his efforts were to no avail.

Cursing a blue streak, the wheelman jumped out of the cab, raised the hood and poked around inside the guts of the engine while another T-Patcher standing behind him held a flash for light, hooding the lens with his hand to reduce its visibility to hostile eyes.

"I was afraid of this," Hot Rod told Captain Cody, now covered with grease and holding up a small cylindrical gizmo connected to a length of ruptured black tubing. "It's the oil pump," he went on. "I'm afraid that the transport's history."

Fucking Brits," Lou Jack cursed, and kicked one of the trucks' mud-spattered front tires.

"To hell with the limeys," Cody returned, sizing up the fact that he and his men were now stranded in the middle of enemy territory. "What do we do now? These here hills are lousy with krauts."

Lou Jack pondered that information for a second, not really needing to be reminded of their tactical situation. Suddenly he was hit with a flash of inspiration.

"We dog-robbed that transport from the Brits, didn't we?" he suggested to Cody. "Well, the krauts have got transport, too, don't they?"

"That's right, Sergeant," Cody returned with a broadening grin. "I believe I'm beginning to see what you're driving at."

18

The scuttled transport had been shoved into a roadside ditch and camouflaged with chopped-down branches. Then the Fifth Platoon, with Sergeant Lou Jack Claymore on point, infiltrated the garrison in the ruined castle they had spotted on their trip up to the monastery.

The T-Patchers didn't need any special drilling on how to infiltrate an enemy base. Faces blackened with mud, they stole across the moonless landscape with the Texas bobcat's natural stealth and the rattler's orneriness and cunning.

As boys the dogfaces of Fifth Platoon had learned how to stalk and ambush prey, learned the deadly skills from their fathers, who'd passed it down from the days of the great westward migration of the early 1800s, when Texas was still a Spanish colony and tribes of Apaches and Comanches and other hostile Indians roamed the land.

As did Lou Jack, Captain Murch Cody ported the specially outfitted M-3 SMGs that Fifth Platoon had brought along on their mission.

They could be damn glad that Cody had managed to lay his hands on the additional special ordnance. As the T-Patchers drew abreast of the garrison's perimeter, the platoon had reason to be thankful for the silenced M-3s they carried.

A two-man perimeter patrol suddenly appeared, their helmets glinting dully in scattered beams of moonlight that came through overcast skies.

The reason that the T-Patchers hadn't spotted the sentries before was that one of the Germans had been in the bushes relieving himself. The other sentry had been sitting atop a fallen log, stealing a smoke, upwind of the Texans by a few score feet.

The one who sat on the log appeared stunned as he noticed the American GIs and jumped to his feet, dropping his cigarette on the pine-needle littered forest floor. He scrabbled to bring the Schmeisser SMG hanging on a strap behind his back to its firing position, but he wasn't nearly fast enough.

Set on semiauto, Lou Jack's silenced M-3 went *sput!-sput!-sput!* in rapid succession as three trigger pulls sent a hellburst of parabellum fire stitching a bloody zigzag from left ear to right shoulder, ripping most of the sentry's head off in the process.

The burst catapulted him backward with his arms flung out, resembling a high diver doing a backflip as he crashed to the ground.

"Klaus, was ist los?" his partner cursed as he emerged from the cover of rustling bushes almost simultaneously with the night kill. His glance fell on Klaus's bloody corpse, and he pivoted in place to stare dumbfounded at Lou Jack. Seeing the American fisting the squat black autoweapon and understanding what had just taken place, the German froze.

"Fill your hand," Lou Jack told him as he let the SMG drop in his fist to a muzzle-downward position. The German unfroze and grabbed for his Schmeisser as Lou Jack raised the M-3 and let him have it across the chest with another silenced autoburst of 124-grain gutbusters. Dragged by the heels of his jackboots, the second sentry joined his playmate in the eternal peace of the surrounding bushes.

With the sentries taken down, Fifth Platoon advanced through the dense shadows, crouch-walking on a carpet of silent pine needles. Hunkering low, they waited until the revolving searchlight beams of the four guard towers at each corner of the fence surrounding the base perimeter passed them by.

Then they produced wire cutters and carefully snipped out a gap in the concertina wire that ringed the perimeter of the Nazi troop garrison after establishing that the fence was not electrified.

"Corrigan, Barton and Bragg, you three stand guard," Lou Jack told his men. "If we're not back in ten minutes, just make tracks back to our lines the best way you can."

When his troops rogered that order, Lou Jack joined the rest of the hard-probe squad as the last man to slide under the fence, moments before one of the revolving searchlight beams swept past his former position on its glaring circuit of the base perimeter.

"I'LL BE a son of a bitch!" Sergeant Lou Jack exclaimed. "I think we hit the jackpot, boys."

Within a ruined structure of the castle's stone outbuildings, which had been partially roofed over with corrugated tin sheeting, the platoon hard-probers located the base's motor pool. Inside the garage were gray-green armored patrol vehicles, four wheels up front, half-tracks behind.

The armored patrol cars were each outfitted with pintle-mounted .50-caliber Browning machine guns. The Brownings were box fed, but the steel ammo boxes that would normally contain the ammo belts appeared to be unfilled.

"Hillihann," Lou Jack said to the squad's wheelman and grease monkey, "check out these half-tracks. Do it on the qt, hear?"

"Gotcha, Sarge," Hot Rod returned with a short nod.

While Hillihann lifted up the engine cowling of the first Mercedes war wagon, Lou Jack volunteered himself a couple of men and went to see what he could do about filling the machine gun's ammo boxes with live .50-caliber rounds.

Keeping well hidden by the shadows of the castle's towering walls, Lou Jack stopped short as he suddenly heard German voices coming his way, laughing and talking. Flattening his body against the side of a building, the SMG buttstock cradled in the crook of his arm, the muzzle parallel with his jawline, Lou Jack held his fingers to his lips. His silenced SMG was at the ready with a 9 mm round already chambered.

Their jackboots crunching on gravel, two German officers passed the T-Patchers without even suspecting their presence on the base. The officers appeared to be all caught up in telling a joke concerning a French prostitute and a soldier's mule and didn't even dream that there were American commandos hiding in their midst.

When the crunch of boot leather on gravel and the sound of voices finally receded, Lou Jack and his squad continued to recce the garrison's compound. They managed to locate the ammo dump a few minutes later. The dump was situated adjacent to the motor pool but was hidden from view behind the single standing wall of a shattered building that had probably once been a stable.

Lou Jack took out the sentry posted to guard the wall with a sound-suppressed autoburst, and his T-Patchers dragged the body out of sight while Lou Jack stood guard with the SMG ready to dispense more whispering death if necessary.

Tossing the T-Patcher his subgun when the body was concealed behind some shop machinery, Lou Jack took a quick look-see around the place. He had little difficulty finding the ammo boxes for the .50s that he had come there to commandeer. Grabbing two crates apiece, Lou Jack's squad set those aside for the present.

Something else had caught his eye, too—German Panzerfausts. The Panzerfausts were single-use versions of the American bazooka. They were easy to shoot, and their 5.95-inch high-explosive warhead packed a devastating wallop. Lou Jack decided to take the Panzerfausts with them, as well, and the squad slung all they could carry over their shoulders by the weapons' carrying straps.

With Hillihann's assurance that the armored cars were all in good operating condition and the Brownings' ammo boxes loaded up with hundreds of rounds each of .50-caliber ammunition, the T-Patchers climbed aboard the commandeered half-tracks.

There was little doubt that their chances of rolling out of the compound unchallenged were small as a cathouse's profits on Christmas Eve. Nevertheless, the chance did exist. The Germans, after all, had no reason to suspect that the Americans had infiltrated their lines, let alone their mountain garrison.

The instant that the staff cars began to roll, though, the T-Patchers' luck changed. Suddenly Klaxons shattered the stillness of the night as a probing searchlight beam from one of the guard towers pinned the lead car in its blinding glare.

From all directions there came the cacophony of shrill voices hollering in German. As Hillihann revved the engine of the lead car, the Germans were already moving in to stop the T-Patchers cold.

19

The earthshaking concussion of a big 81 mm mortar shell-burst cratered the earth only a few feet from the front tires of the lead patrol car. The ferocious impact hurled the chassis of the war wagon clear off the muddy surface of the mountain roadbed.

Multiple rifle-grenade strikes joined the deadly chorus of exploding munitions, throwing up gouts of road gravel and flame here and there along the path of the fast-moving patrol cars. The accuracy of the German fire was probably owed to the glaring beams of the searchlight beacons shining down from the guard tower strung along the base perimeter.

Signaling to BAR-man Robertson, Murch Cody made it clear that he wanted that mean eye put out. Flashing the officer the high sign, Private Robertson shouldered the autorifle he could handle as well as his own right arm.

Even from the wildly lurching, speedballing staff car, Robertson's fire was accurate. The burning eye of the beacon winked out instantly as a fusillade of .30-caliber steel shattered its lens to jagged bits and dimmed the glowing filament within.

In the second armored patrol wagon, Private Blackroot hunkered behind the big, belt-fed Browning. The T-Patcher rifleman clutched the spade grips of the heavy-barreled machine gun in sure hands as he swung the autoweapon around on its 360-degree firing axis and aimed at the next of the remaining crow's nests through the machine gun's pancake gunsights.

The BAR weapon chattered menacingly, spitting brass casings from its ejection port as a lashing scorpion tail of glowing silver .50-caliber tracers whipped skyward and stitched jaggedly across the second searchlight beacon.

All at once, the lancing death beam of the searchlight lurched to one side as the German sentry behind it toppled thirty feet from the crow's nest to break every bone in his body on the rocky ground below.

Suddenly Blackroot gave out a holler and sat down heavily behind the machine gun, drilled through the side of the head by a lucky round from a gun fired by one of the Germans spilling out of barracks buildings along the route of the three fleeing cars.

There were still two functional searchlights left, in any case. Their blinding beams continued to track the armored column like the furies of hell.

From the guard towers positioned high above, fresh pulses of .50-caliber autofire lashed out savagely as a replacement climbed the unmanned sentry tower and got behind the machine gun in the crow's nest, tracking the weapon down on the lead escape car and snarling as he pulled the trigger.

Cussing a blue streak, Lou Jack took the dead T-Patcher's place behind the upended heavy machine gun. Swinging the down-pointing barrel upward again, he pointed it toward one of the crow's nests with its glowing, menacing light.

That burning spot mocked his men as it pinned them like insects in its blinding glare, belching out ugly yellow flame-tongues and stuttering white-hot steel to harass them in their flight.

Lou Jack was sick and tired of it. Squeezing his fists tight on the Browning's spade grips and sighting through the center of the weapon's pancake gunsight, the T-Patcher sergeant sent a vortexing whirlwind of heavy-caliber answering studs screaming up toward the Nazi gunner stationed in the sentry post at three o'clock.

Every single bullet scored a hit as Lou Jack poured on the firepower, cursing and laughing with glee. The miniature sun of the hot light burst to flinders with a loud, soul-satisfying pop! and winked out forever. The gimlet eye of death had now been finally blinded.

In the juddering rear of the captured war wagon in the lead, Captain Murch Cody had jettisoned the sound-suppressor attachment of his M-3 machine pistol. Now Cody was firing the ratcheting autoweapon in one hand while he blasted away with his general-issue Colt .45 pistol in the other.

As good as the Texans were with their hand cannons, though, the small-arms fire they were currently trading wasn't nearly a match for the concentrated firepower that the enemy were capable of bringing to bear on the fleeing vehicles at a moment's notice. Without doing something to even the score, the pissing contest would go on until the numbers on the other side decided the outcome of the fight in favor of the Hun.

Now that both pistols had run dry, Cody threw down the SMG and Colt automatic and grabbed one of the Panzerfausts that the T-Patcher probe crew had promoted from the garrison's ammo dump.

Time to end the pissing contest.

Arming the Panzerfaust by pulling the cocking level on the side of the firing tube toward him, he aimed the bulb-ended projectile tip of the weapon at the armored carrier near the base's fenced-off forecourt. Even as he did, the carrier was raising its cannon to throw an 80 mm shell at them.

The Panzerfaust in his hands kicked like a mule and breathed fire like a dragon as the high-explosive warhead exited the pipe on its short, deadly journey.

The 5.95-inch round scored a direct hit, the powerful blast of its spherical explosive charge piercing the armor of the tracked war wagon and immediately making it burst into flames.

As coughing and vomiting storm troopers spilled out of the burning wreckage of the armored half-track, Cody launched a second Panzerfaust killstrike at the garrison's fuel dump that his vehicle was just now passing.

The stacked drums of flammable high-octane tank fuel ignited with a gigantic whoosh and a deafening explosion that produced such fierce blast waves that Cody was almost hurled over the side of the open patrol car.

The German base was totally convulsed with the screams of the dying and the staccato reports of small-arms fire and exploding enemy ordnance as the first of the speeding escape vehicles reached the perimeter fence that gave access to the road outside.

At the main gate of the base, there stood a sentry box. The sentry box was manned by a trio of men in field gray greatcoats who had taken up defensive positions with Schmeisser submachine guns armed and ready.

One of them let fly a Panzerfaust round at Cody's car. Behind the wheel of the lead vehicle, Hillihann swerved in a sudden evasive maneuver. The Panzerfaust warhead flew wide of its intended mark and detonated harmlessly off to one side in a shower of fire, but the next shot was not likely to miss.

The driver poured on the steam while Lou Jack whirled the BAR machine gun in the second escape car toward the German sentry position and began firing over the head of his driver while his own body acted as counterweight to the big, chattering gun.

Swinging the barrel back and forth, not giving a tinker's damn if the weapon's perforated barrel was overheating and in danger of cooking off the ammo supply in its receiver, Lou Jack poured sustained autofire at the Germans in Fifth Platoon's path to freedom.

He was rewarded by the sight of them flinging up their arms and doing blood-spurting marionette dances as the lead vehicle crashed through the garrison's main gate and bucked like a rodeo bronc. First the front, then the rear tires found purchase on the road that wound past the base.

Fishtailing and flinging up huge gouts of mud and gravel as it speedballed from the hell-visited garrison, the second patrol car stopped to pick up the three T-Patchers who had been posted outside the breach in the perimeter fence. Before gunning their engines and tearing down the road, the line of stolen staff cars pulled up abreast of the shattered and burning main gate, and the T-Patchers grabbed up all the unused Panzerfausts.

On Murch Cody's signal, Fifth Platoon launched a massed barrage of Panzerfaust warheads into the base perimeter, raining yet more fire and death down on Hitler's bloody swastika as their parting shot.

20

Major General Hoagland, commander of the T-Patchers, was fit to chew the rug.

Only the fact that Cody and his men had succeeded in causing severe damage to a German garrison—and bringing back an item of critical military Intelligence in the bargain—had saved Cody and Lou Jack from being busted down in rank to apprentice latrine cleaners and the rest of Fifth Platoon from sitting out the rest of the war in the company guardhouse.

"Of all the ill-considered, ill-planned and just plain chickenshit stunts, this is the most ridiculous I've ever heard of," he shouted at Cody. "Why in the name of Sam Hill didn't you come to me with this Intelligence?" Hoagland demanded, pointing his finger at the captain.

"Sir, there just wasn't time," he replied coolly. "I've already explained to you about the, uh, special circumstances."

"Yes, the circumstances," Hoagland blustered, cutting Cody off with a wave of a cigar-clutching hand before he could say another word. "A kindly old priest who was shepherding a most unusual flock—a brothel full of *whores,* for chrissakes!—just happens to ask you and your men to assist him in transporting sacred relics of his order behind German lines."

"That's right, sir," Cody returned, trying with great difficulty not to sound sheepish.

"Didn't you ever stop to think that there was something highly unusual about the story?"

"Well, sir, with all due respect, you can't deny that we *did* get the letter from the abbot of Cassino by way of Abbot Angelo," Cody explained.

"Ah, yes, the letter," Hoagland told him. "That's another matter. G-2 isn't completely sure that the so-called letter from the abbot of Cassino is legitimate."

"The hell it's not legitimate, sir," Cody blurted out angrily, then added, "You don't mean to tell me that they aren't taking the letter seriously, do you, General?"

Hoagland sat on the edge of his desk, waving off an aide who had cracked the door and reminded him that a reporter from the International Press Syndicate was waiting impatiently to interview him for a feature article.

After telling the aide to send in the newshound in five minutes, Hoagland went on. "I don't make those decisions. As far as operations of this magnitude go, they tend to take on a life and a momentum of their own. I guess I don't have to tell you that Ike's been under a lot of pressure to give the order to bomb Cassino. Your message from the abbot, I'm sorry to say, is just one more piece of paper on his desk."

"Shit, General," Cody exclaimed, "what the hell kind of a show are we running here, anyway?"

The general continued to ignore the captain's insubordinate tone, understanding how a good soldier might feel cheated under the circumstances. He merely nodded in understanding by way of answer, but didn't say anything else.

"Look, Captain," Hoagland said finally, now in a milder voice. "I was young once myself. I frankly don't know whether to hold mass courts-martial or put you and your men in for citations for bravery and initiative under fire. Let's just leave matters as they stand, for the time being."

"Yes, sir," Cody said edgily. "Orders are orders, sir."

Without responding, the general hit a button on his desk intercom, telling his aide to send the newspaperman in, signaling to Cody that their meeting was over.

As Cody turned to leave, he got a look at the reporter who was coming in. The newsman was as tall as Cody and wore the wrinkled fatigues and mud-caked boots of a line-doggie, except that he carried no weapon. The blue patch on his shoulder identified him as a member of the press corps. For some reason the sight of the guy gave Cody the same sensation he always had whenever turning over a rock and finding a diamondback rattler coiled beneath it.

"By the way, Captain Cody," General Hoagland said as Cody reached for the knob of the office door, "I'd like you to meet Mike Jakeway of the International Press Syndicate. I'm sure you've read his newspaper reports from Salerno and Anzio."

"Sure, I have," Cody said, extending his hand and shaking the newshound's. "Pleased to meet you." Jakeway had a firm handshake, all right, but there was something about the guy that creeped Cody out just the same.

When he was finally outside in the sunbaked street, he was glad to be out of Jakeway's presence. Cody shrugged. Call it intuition, but his gut feeling was that Jakeway was bad news, in more ways than one.

LOU JACK and some of the T-Patchers of Fifth Platoon were sitting around an outdoor table at the town's only restaurant, drinking beer and straight grappa.

A company jeep pulled up suddenly with a squeal of hastily applied brakes. Captain Cody hopped out of the cab and handed Lou Jack a carbon copy of a dispatch that had just come in from divisional headquarters in Naples.

"Don't ask me how I promoted this copy," he told him. "Just get a squint at what it says."

The sergeant read the dispatch, as other T-Patchers clustered around to read over the NCO's shoulder. Nodding when he was finished, Lou Jack passed it along to his anxious men.

"Son of a bitch," he cussed, shaking his head. "After all we went through."

The dispatch read that earlier that morning, elements of the 142nd and 143rd Infantry Divisions had attempted to cross the Rapido Rover, which flowed past the foot of Monte Cassino.

At least a battalion of Wehrmacht troops were dug in on the opposite bank in force. Heavily entrenched, they had poured obliterating firepower on the Americans who had attempted to cross the Rapido.

Almost two thousand T-Patchers were mowed down by hot German lead in what turned out to be nothing less than an outright massacre.

Dazed and broken by their experience, the survivors of the ill-fated river crossing had all described the same impression: the unshakable conviction that hostile German eyes were peering down at them from behind the dark windows of the abbey that sat at the top of the rocky peak of Mount Cassino.

"They'll bomb the bejesus out of the place for sure now," Lou Jack said to Cody.

"Uh-huh," Cody returned with a grim nod of assent as he folded up the dispatch and slid it back into his pocket. "And kill a lot of other good men when all along the brass could have avoided the mountain entirely."

"Have a drink with your men, Cody," Lou Jack told the captain, pushing the half-empty bottle of grappa toward him across the tabletop.

"What the hell do we drink to, Sergeant?" Cody asked Lou Jack, already reaching for the bottle of Kickapoo Joy Juice.

"To the sorry-assed dogfaces of the Thirty-Sixth Infantry," Lou Jack said after only a moment's consideration. "To the mud-spattered, belly-crawlin', blood-covered patron saints of humanity's lost causes."

BOOK THREE:
No-Man's-Land

Rome-Arno Campaign,
March to July, 1944

21

Valmontone

On the outskirts of Rome, the thunder and boom of the big howitzers in the rear was a sound that was as familiar to each dogface as the beating of his own heart.

The din of the big 105s constantly hammering German defensive positions had become hardly noticeable to the GIs who had slogged up the boot of Italy from the bloody killing grounds of Salerno and Anzio months before.

The thudding of the big guns didn't bother men who knew that the sound was a death rattle for the enemy.

Soon the T-Patchers would be in Rome, sitting pretty. Valmontone was the final way station before the Army rolled in with the infantry leading the wedge of fighting men and combat machinery.

The long, grueling months of knee-deep mud and wholesale slaughter had taught even the brass hats a hard-learned lesson about the enemy they had come three thousand miles to wipe off the face of the earth.

Hitler's legions played rough and dirty. In order to prevail against their kind, the fight against them had to be even harder and dirtier.

At Salerno the assault formations of the Thirty-Sixth Infantry Division had been butchered like pigs corralled in a slaughterhouse because the beachhead had not been softened up with saturated artillery fire prior to the U.S. landing.

At Anzio the same mistake had been avoided, but the order to dig in rather than move up the coast straight toward Rome had allowed Kesselring's forces to entrench themselves with even bloodier consequences for U.S. infantry personnel.

These mistakes would not be repeated in the taking of Rome. Ike and his joint chiefs of staff knew full well that Hitler was sure to be betting his cards on Allied reluctance to bomb a mostly civilian population whose fighting men had surrendered so quickly that the conquering troops had practically to hand out numbers.

These same troops were now joining their former enemies in droves on the front lines against Hitler's badly mauled Wehrmacht legions. Eisenhower knew that and many things besides, but in the end he had finally bowed to necessity and chosen American military lives over those of Italian civilians.

Rome had been bombed, but it hadn't been an all-out effort by any means. The sorties of fully loaded B-29s had spared what they could—under direct orders to avoid the Colosseum, the Forum of the Caesars and other similar architectural features of historical and/or cultural importance—but their primary objective had been to smash the Nazi war machine to dust and ashes and to insure in the process that no fresh combat troops would await American GIs when they went in and took the city.

With Allied artillery constantly thundering as the big guns pounded German targets closer, closer and ever closer to Rome itself, the infantry that had fought so hard to take the German Winter Line and the Liri Valley beyond it advanced northward along Highway 6—the first army to do so in fifteen hundred years. Though the Germans continued to fight hard, even valiantly, contesting every mile that the Allies reclaimed, the rest was anticlimax.

Valmontone, an ancient Roman town situated only a few miles outside of Rome, had fallen after the kind of dirty, close-in fighting that had characterized most of the encounters between German and American infantry in the battle to take the towns along the road to Rome.

Field hospitals had been set up, latrines dug and the swastika flag of Hitler's boastfully christened Thousand-Year Reich had come down at Wehrmacht command posts to be replaced by the Stars and Stripes, the Union Jack and the Tricolor of the Free French Forces.

As the towns changed hands, in one way the local Italian populace felt much the same toward the advancing Allied armies as they had felt about their former German overseers: they were in a hurry for their unwanted guests to leave.

Soon the recently arrived American infantry troops would do precisely that. For several weeks now, more and more troops from the rear echelons had been arriving at Valmontone, a principal American staging area for the final Allied push into the Eternal City.

So far the troop buildup had been a classic case of the hurry-up-and-wait syndrome that had plagued much of U.S. combat planning during the war, however much the line troops had learned to resign themselves to it.

Hurry up and wait meant that one minute American dogfaces had been trying to forget the war behind the lines in Naples or Sicily, but the next, they found themselves immediately ordered to the front.

Having finally arrived there, they were then instructed to sit on their behinds and wait for the order to board transports to the front that came down from the brass hats of Allied command.

Among the many other infantry units summoned to Valmontone to take part in the final phase of the war in southern Italy was Easy Company, which, along with other elements of the Thirty-Sixth Infantry Division, would form the spearhead of the advance on Rome.

As much as they'd hated being torn away from the booze, broads, gambling and other diversions of rough-and-ready Naples, the T-Patchers felt proud to be part of the spearhead—not to get first crack at the dames and the hooch as some had charged, but because their selection for this important duty meant that they were among the very best their superiors could throw at Hitler's minions.

Like most of the American fighting men who had come overseas to see combat in a European land war, the T-Patchers had started out with little or no firsthand experience with Hitler, Nazism or the German infantry soldier.

Most had held few gripes against them, either, except for the purely intellectual variety that accompanied the outrage that a breed who valued freedom as much as Texans did felt for those whose philosophy it was to take it away from others weaker than themselves.

All of that had changed at Salerno, Anzio, in the baptism by blood and fire of the mud-cursed Aurunci and a thousand other combat hellzones the T-Patchers had encountered on their long, relentless march toward Rome.

Now, finally poised on the brink of the assault on the Eternal City, the T-Patchers had taken the full measure of the German fighting man and had learned to both respect and despise him. The T-Patchers had witnessed firsthand the cruelty of the German soldier.

They had witnessed the cold, calculating manner with which he dispatched his sanguine duties. They had learned firsthand of the treachery of which the savage spawn of Hitler's bloody Reich was capable, and this knowledge had become part of their grim determination to win the battle at any cost.

The dogfaces of the Thirty-Sixth had changed, too. The second-line combat troops of the Texas National Guard who had been flung as green recruits onto the unforgiving sands of Salerno and Anzio had grown hard and grimly motivated. Fear had been purged from them by fire and steel, and they now fought with a single-minded vengeance that only those who know themselves to be living on borrowed time can bring to the field of battle.

Rome or hell, killing or dying, it didn't matter a damn which. The T-Patchers were ready, willing and able to wade into the thick of the fighting and kick the Hun back to Berlin and straight to blazes.

22

To an observer not familiar with the conditions on the Italian front, Bobby and Jimmy looked like two stumblebums as they leaned against a wall of the ruins of what had formerly been a homey Italian pensione.

Their faces were unshaven, their fatigues were filthy and their eyes stared out at the world with a hollow look. There was one important difference between the two dogfaces and the Italian civilians, though. The GI knew where his next meal was coming from. The locals didn't.

Bobby and Jimmy sat amid a group of other Easy Company T-Patchers who were waiting for transports that would shuttle them to the front lines only a couple of miles away along Highway 6.

Like the rest of the unit, they had been cooling their heels for days. The only thing to do, aside from getting clipped by the Italians dealing booze, nylons, girlie magazines and other necessities on the black market, was to catch up on their reading.

Trouble was, apart from *Stars and Stripes,* there were no other papers available, except for the local Italian ones. Since most of the T-Patchers couldn't even pronounce "spaghetti" correctly, their only other reading matter consisted of tattered and dog-eared papers mailed from home, which were as out-of-date as they were worn-out.

"Hey, listen to this," Bobby sang out, shaking his head angrily. "It says here that 'minor patrol action and comparative quiet continue on the Italian front, with no progress reported.' The douchebag who wrote this crap is lower than any kraut in my book."

"Lemme have a gander at this," Jimmy growled, grabbing the tattered newsprint and reading it with the same shakes of his head that Bobby had just displayed. "Jeez, the piss-ant responsible for this garboia probably never even came anywhere near the front. Probably got his info from gazing into the hole in his dick."

Across the rubble-strewn street, Private Rusty-Lee Magruder licked the tip of a pencil and held it hovering over a V-Mail blank as he contemplated what to write his sweetheart Laurie-Ann in Laredo.

Rusty-Lee hadn't heard from Laurie-Ann since Cassino, and had lately started to worry about her faithfulness to him. But the mail being what it was, he'd got a half-dozen letters in Naples after being sent to the rear, all of them from his fiancée.

Like many another GI, Rusty-Lee's problem was that most of what a line-doggie had to say consisted of describing his experiences at the front, and the T-Patcher knew well that the military censors would cut any such letter to shreds. Rusty-Lee scratched his head, stuck for an opening line.

Suddenly the scattered T-Patchers looked up just in time to see a jeep pull up with the company clerk's insignia emblazoned on its sides. Stump Billings was fat and dumb, but he delivered the mail and that was enough to make the sight of him a welcome one to the T-Patchers.

Seeing that mail call was imminent, and glad for a break in the monotony of their wait at the front, the grungy T-Patchers shuffled from their scattered positions to meet the mail jeep.

Rusty-Lee heard his name called and tucked his V-Mail blank into the pocket of his fatigue jacket. The new letter he'd just received was also from Laurie-Ann. Rusty-Lee sat down on a big hunk of rubble, unfolded the letter and read it eagerly.

As he scanned the page, his heart froze and his blood boiled. It was a Dear John letter. Laurie-Ann said that she was engaged to a guy who worked at a munitions factory screwing proximity fuses into artillery shells. She'd met him at a victory picnic. And, well, they were in love.

She added that she hoped that Rusty-Lee would understand her newfound happiness and respect her wishes, and also hoped that he would be okay and not do anything stupid or reckless because of her actions and that she still thought about him and would continue to remember him in her prayers.

"Hey, izzat a letter from your girl?" asked one of the T-Patchers as Rusty-Lee finished reading. Rusty-Lee looked up slowly from the letter and stared at the dogface expressionlessly. His lips were motionless and his eyes were as blank as a freshly whitewashed concrete wall. "What's the matter?" the doughfoot asked him. "You sick or something?"

Without saying another word, Rusty-Lee hauled off with his best Sunday punch and belted the questioner straight in the stomach. The short right jab bowled the inquisitive GI over like a ninepin hit by a strike. A couple of other T-Patchers nearby rushed to the scene and helped the hurt soldier to his feet.

"Hey, why'd you do that for?" one of them asked Rusty-Lee. But Rusty-Lee didn't hear the shouted question. As he turned and trudged away, he dropped the letter from his former fiancée in a bomb crater filled with greasy black water.

Then he stomped off away from the T-Patchers' position, letting the V-Mail blank float on the scummy surface. One of the T-Patchers retrieved the letter from the waterlogged shell crater. A brief scan was enough to tell the whole tale of what had ticked Rusty-Lee off.

As the men clustered around the dogface who was now holding Rusty-Lee's discarded Dear John letter, shaking their heads and commenting on how only a dame could do something this rotten to a guy at the front, they didn't pay much attention to the whine of a jeep engine grinding toward them.

The driver of the jeep had to honk the horn repeatedly in order to get the attention of the head-shaking and cursing dogfaces, and then it was only given grudgingly.

"Tennnnn-*hut*!" somebody sounded off at the sight of an officer.

"All right, you goldbricks, as you were," shouted Easy Company's commanding officer, Captain Murch Cody, who had stepped from the jeep's running board.

Had it been any other officer, the dogfaces might have given him a somewhat different reception, especially in light of the ill feelings produced by the explosive combination of heel cooling and Dear Johning. But the T-Patchers knew that Cody had seen as much hard combat time as any man among them. Besides, he was as much a Texan as any of them were, and as such was entitled to their undivided attention.

"You sorry-assed bozos in Second Platoon are getting yourselves a new dance partner," Cody went on, while all eyes were turned on the civilian who was standing beside Cody. "Men, I'd like to introduce you to Mr. Mike Jakeway of the International Press Syndicate. As a noncombatant observer, Jakeway here will accompany you gutless, mother-lovin' wonders as you enter the city of Rome, and I want you all to extend him your fullest cooperation."

If Cody'd had his druthers, he would just as soon have sent the IPS war correspondent over to some other outfit. As far as he was concerned, civilians had no damn business accompanying front-line troops into a combat zone.

That went double for reporters, who were not much better than leeches and cockroaches in Cody's book. It went triple for Jakeway, to whom he'd taken an instant dislike the second he'd lain eyes on him in Valmontone. But General Hoagland himself had insisted that Jakeway was the captain's responsibility and had issued his instructions in the form of a direct order.

Not only didn't he take much to the notion of a noncom who made his living off writing about how the men around him died, but, unlike Cody's T-Patchers, Jakeway could—and ultimately would—also be able to walk away from the battlefield to some cushy desk back home when he got a bellyful of fighting. That was a privilege that none of his men—or himself for that matter—shared with the civilian newsman.

But quite apart from anything else, Cody just plain didn't care for Jakeway personally. In the brief space of time they had been acquainted, the newshound had displayed a propensity for making a man feel like he was a bug under a magnifying glass, a thing to be studied and then thrown away.

Cody could tell that this East Coast dude was a hustler, out for himself and himself alone. Cody didn't want to foist Jakeway on Second Platoon, but regrettably he didn't have any choice in the matter.

The T-Patchers themselves would have to make up their own minds about what to do about Jakeway. Cody's one consolation was the knowledge that in Second Platoon, Jakeway would find men who had no scruples about giving a phoney the treatment he justly deserved—and regulations be damned.

As CODY HANDED OFF Jakeway to Second Platoon, in the Thirty-Sixth Division field hospital situated on the opposite end of the town of Valmontone, other members of the platoon were standing at the bedside of a GI patient.

Private Francis "Big Butch" Bowermeister had got hit in the rump by shrapnel in the fight to take the town. Next to a hot date with Lana Turner, it was the one thing that every GI dreamed about but seldom received—the classic "million-dollar wound," a one-way, all-expenses-paid ticket back home.

Privates Wheats Dimmock, Jo-Jo DiPalma and Louis "Jackass" Jacquess watched the ward nurse come over to Bowermeister's bedside. They already knew her name: Nurse O'Toole. It had already become Nurse *Oh-Oh-Oh-Toole* and sometimes just plain *Ohhhh-Toole* once they had left the confines of the hospital ward.

Whatever her name, the nurse in question was a pretty, blond native of Dublin, Ireland, who was built like a pinup girl—all lovely womanhood with the capability to bring life to men half-dead. Nurse O'Toole smiled at the three grungy dogfaces who ogled her fine physique, well highlighted by her snug nurse's uniform. Nurse O'Toole knew these particular T-Patchers by sight. They had visited her patient before.

"Top o' the mornin' to you, boys," she said to the leering dogfaces. Bending slightly forward, Nurse O'Toole jammed a fever thermometer into Bowermeister's mouth and took his temperature. Bowermeister rolled his eyes and grabbed for Nurse O'Toole's rear end. She slapped his hand away and smoothed down her white uniform dress.

"Not half-bad," she told Bowermeister as she removed the thermometer. "No fever today. Your wound's healing well."

"Yeah, but I got a strange pain," Bowermeister protested. "See, it's down here." He pointed toward his crotch. "It keeps throbbin', like. Can you help me, Nurse Ohhhh-Toole?"

Such talk would have earned the likes of Bowermeister a smart rap in his chops if she were in her native Dublin. But this wasn't Dublin, and men like Bowermeister who faced terrible death every day rated a bit more tolerance.

"Oh," she said in her Irish brogue, "I'm sure some fine broth of an Italian girl will be happy to take care of that pain when you're discharged, Private," she answered. Saying that, Nurse O'Toole left the ward, her backside swinging enticingly, earning her share of wolf whistles from other GIs lying along the rows of beds.

"Jesus, what an ass," Jackass said admiringly. "She makes Betty Grable look like a Girl Scout."

"Watch what you say about Betty Grable, wise guy," Wheats shot back, flashing an angry look. "She's my good-luck charm."

"Whaddaya mean?" Jo-Jo asked.

Wheats took off his helmet and pulled something out from underneath it. Jo-Jo and Jackass saw that it was a tattered picture of Betty Grable that he'd clipped from a movie magazine. Wheats kissed the photo and carefully tucked it back inside his helmet.

"Anyway, she sure is fine," Wheats put in, referring to Nurse O'Toole. "You getting any action, there, old buddy?" he concluded to Bowermeister, who now lay with his hands propped beneath his head.

"Fellas, all I'm gonna tell you is that I'm a happy man," Bowermeister confided to his buddies with a wink. "After the lights in this ward go out, the nights are no longer cold and lonely for this infantry soldier."

"Get outa here, Bowermeister," Jo-Jo exclaimed. "You really making time with that stacked Irish blonde?"

"Would I lie to my buddies?" Bowermeister asked with a smile. The T-Patchers let that one pass.

"Anyway, you got lucky, Bowermeister. That's for sure," Wheats offered. "We'll be moving out into Rome pretty soon while you'll be laid up nice and cozy here. By the time you're back out again, the war in Italy'll probably be over and done with."

"That's where you're wrong," Bowermeister returned as he tossed back the blanket that covered him, revealing that he was dressed in ODs from the waist down and wearing mud-caked combat boots. "I'm coming with you."

"Bowermeister, get the hell back into bed before the medics see you and throw you into the booby hatch!" they warned. But Bowermeister was already pulling on a shirt he'd taken from under his mattress and grabbing up other gear that he'd stashed in a footlocker by his bed.

"Let's get a move on," he told his platoon buddies. "We're getting back to the unit. My daddy raised me to finish what I started, especially when it comes to a fight."

23

The Appian Way

Easy Company's Second Platoon was discharged from a ten-wheeled transport truck onto the ancient road to Rome. Now part of Italy's Highway 6, the Via Cassilina had been employed as an invasion route toward the Eternal City by soldiers since the time of Hannibal, and for centuries before that.

Nobody but the U.S. Army had succeeded in taking it all the way in, however, in the past fifteen hundred years or so.

The highway ran through the suburbs on the city's outskirts, which were still held by pockets of Germans covering the rear flanks of the retreating Wehrmacht.

Heavily entrenched, pockets of Wehrmacht and SS personnel were making life hard on the steadily advancing Americans as they drew their net closed. Rome would not change hands just yet, or quite that easily.

Even as they scrambled from their canvas-covered transport, dodging for cover amid the caved-in wreckage of bombed-out buildings, the T-Patchers came under sudden attack. From their deadly nests amid the twisted girders and concrete wreckage of an apartment block directly ahead, German machine gunners sent fire chattering their way.

The entire front wall of the apartment building nearest the T-Patchers had taken a hit and fallen away, leaving three walls standing and exposing the boxlike superstructure of gigantic concrete slabs and the skeleton of steel I-beams. The machine gunners were positioned here and there within the honeycomb of ruined floors.

From their lofty vantage points, the Germans were sitting pretty. They had set up machine gun emplacements capable of pouring down crucifying fire on any units passing across the turf they controlled.

Here, as had been the case in virtually every encounter of the Italian campaign, the Germans, who had consistently enjoyed the tactical advantage, were not giving ground easily.

Not five minutes after disembarking from the transport, Second Platoon took its first casualty. Chancing a run across no-man's-land toward his buddies' position behind the cover of a kind of sunken playground, Jo-Jo DiPalma was walloped across the shoulders, caught in the chest by a fusillade of German steel from the death-spitting guns above.

The impact of the heavy-caliber rounds lifted his legs off the ground as he ran toward cover. For a moment he hung suspended in the air, then Jo-Jo fell flat on his face and skidded in the dirt, half rolling with outflung arms to stare at the gunmetal gray sky with sightless eyes.

"Cover me."

Tears came to Bowermeister's eyes as he saw what had happened to Jo-Jo.

"You're crazy, man. Don't even think about it," Jackass told him, hunkering in the shell hole beside Bowermeister.

"I said cover me." Bowermeister's set jaw and burning eyes left no room for argument.

As his buddies lay down suppressing fire, Bowermeister challenged enemy fire to get to his dead friend. Breaking from cover, he snapped off bursts from his .45 automatic and dodged across the open space of no-man's-land with lead kicking at his boot heels.

Somehow Bowermeister succeeded in dragging Jo-Jo's bullet-riddled remains toward his unit's position. Cleaning the blood from Jo-Jo's sightless eyes, he removed his battle-stained dog tags, his Army-issue wristwatch and his wallet. As saddened as Bowermeister was about his buddy's death, he even less liked the prospect of writing to break the bad news to Jo-Jo's widow and young son back in Wichita Falls.

Platoon leader Sergeant Matt "Jaybird" Macon chose that moment to spring over to their position, diving from shell hole to shell hole to get to his men and stay clear of flying Krupp shrapnel.

Pushing his steel-pot helmet back on his head, he said, "Sorry about Jo-Jo. But we're pinned down here, ladies and gents. I put in a request for mortar support. When the rounds hit, get ready to move." Saying that, Macon broke and ran to the next pocket of T-Patchers to issue them identical orders.

Suddenly another figure was crouching beside Bowermeister. The grieving T-Patcher felt an immediate sense of disgust overwhelm him.

"Buddy of yours?" asked Mike Jakeway, the IPS war correspondent. Bowermeister nodded and said "uh-huh," then turned away. He didn't feel like talking to the reporter about it just then. Jakeway pressed on, though, unwilling to let it slide.

Jakeway didn't feel the least bit guilty about performing his job. It was the Germans, after all, who had wasted the dogface, not him. His job was to tell the world about it.

"Mind giving me a few words on your feelings right now, soldier?" Jakeway asked. He already had his spiral-topped reporter's notebook out and had flipped to a blank page, licked the tip of his pencil and got ready to write it down for the folks back home.

Bowermeister let out a vicious oath, looking the man squarely in the eyes. Jakeway blinked but otherwise didn't change expression. The machine guns continued to chatter in the background.

"Okay," Jakeway said after a long beat, flipping closed his book. "I understand."

He slunk away to another section of the sunken playground where the platoon had taken refuge from German lead. Hell, he had the material he needed for his story, anyway. He was already composing the moving lament of one hard-bitten Texas cowboy for his fallen comrade in arms. It would be the kind of copy, he knew, that his editor would pounce on greedily.

THE FIRST THUNDEROUS STRIKES of the mortar barrage called in by Sergeant Jaybird Macon hammered away at the enemy position in the ruined apartment complex.

The rounds were new 4.2 mm high-explosive and phosphorous bomblets. They were fired by a chemical mortar battalion in the Allied rear near Roccasecca. The incendiary mortar strikes produced instant chaos amid the German ranks.

A direct hit scored by one of the incendiaries in a machine-gun emplacement instantly set men aflame. Their greatcoats on fire, burning with the nauseating stench of ignited rayon, human torches ran crazily in every direction.

Their screams were frozen in their dying throats, their arms windmilled crazily as the Wehrmacht shooters flung themselves to the concrete deck and thrashed in terminal spasms before blackening to unrecognizable crisps.

Then the mortar squad started throwing in the heavy-duty stuff—80 mm high-explosive rounds that sent thick clouds of pulverized masonry belching in choking clouds that blossomed into the gray, rain-swollen sky in a death-black pall. As the mortars thudded home to devastating effect, German firing petered out, then died away entirely.

"Shake it! Shake it! Shake it, you sorry-assed sons of bitches! Move the hell out!" the T-Patchers heard Sergeant Jaybird Macon shout out.

Hollering battle cries passed down by their forefathers who had taken on Santa Ana's troops on the banks of the San Antonio River, the Texas army was running hell-bent for leather toward the enemy across a field of broken, shattered earth that had stopped being no-man's-land.

Just as Second Platoon ran scrambling from their positions, the platoon's top kick turned in time to see the IPS newshound come jumping out of the shelter of a nearby bomb crater in which he'd been holed up with a group of GIs. No sooner had Jakeway scooted from the crater than the shell hole received a direct hit from a German mortar.

Despite the bloody, blazing hell erupting around him, a dumbfounded Macon stood frozen in his tracks for a long moment. That lucky strike was a one-in-a-million chance. Other members of the platoon had seen what had happened too as they beelined it toward the now remanned machine-gun nests.

In that one blinding instant of fate, the IPS man had immediately gone from being merely a scumbag and a blood-sucking leech. Now Jakeway was something much worse. Something that would insure his being treated worse than a leper with nasal hair from here on in. The mortar strike had branded the civilian reporter the worst of all possible things.

Jakeway had become a battlefield jinx.

PRIVATE RUSTY-LEE MAGRUDER was on point. Ever since receiving his Dear John letter at mail call back in Valmontone, all he could think about was killing, murdering and otherwise exterminating the enemy. The brass hats had shipped him overseas to wipe out the Hun, and that's exactly what he was aiming to do.

The meandering streets of Rome were interspersed with ancient Roman ruins. The ruins provided natural cover for German gun emplacements. Because the ruins were to be found everywhere, on the sides of broad avenues, fenced-off behind modern buildings, the sector of the city was like a hornet's nest of entrenched German positions.

In one such position nearby, a machine gun squad lay protected by a wall of sandbags behind an unmarked ruin that had been a temple to the goddess Minerva almost two thousand years before.

Time-stained frescoes on the walls of ancient marble depicted how the spear-throwing goddess exacted bloody retribution on the foes of her devotees by cutting off their heads and hacking off their limbs and genitalia.

Neither the Germans nor Rusty-Lee were aware of the irony of their situation, or that, more than two thousands years later, they were still serving the Roman goddess's bloody designs. Their only concern in the extreme situation was to kill each other as quickly and as efficiently as possible, and survive to kill yet again.

Rusty-Lee carried grenades hanging from the pullrings of their cotter pins that were slung from chest and shoulder webbing. He ripped them off two at a time and hurled them in bunches toward the chattering machine-gun nest while he ducked behind the protection of a nearby stone wall.

As soon as he heard the combined explosions of the TNT-filled Mills grenades, Rusty-Lee sprinted from cover, spraying fire from his Tommy gun at the Germans.

Fast and lucky, the T-Patcher caught both of them across the abdomen with a single burst of fire. They did spastic, jerky puppet dances and came to a flopping end, hanging over the iron balcony surrounding the sunken ruins.

Unfortunately for Rusty-Lee, he did not notice that one of them was not quite dead. Still having enough life left in him to clutch his Schmeisser's grip in shaking, bloody hands, the dying man squeezed off a burst. It blew away most of Rusty-Lee's right shoulder blade, lung and section of rib cage they were attached to, just before the German dropped dead with a smile of triumph on his face.

Rusty-Lee was able to stumble for another few dozen yards before he finally collapsed across the rim of the dry cistern of a marble fountain and stared at the sky through fast-dimming eyes. He smiled as he saw his fiancée's, Laurie-Ann's, face hover across his darkening field of vision.

"I-I love you," he said through blood-foaming lips. "I-I love you L-Laurie—"

The rest of Rusty-Lee's words were cut off by the crack of a pistol shot that blew away most of this throat and lower jaw.

"*Amerikanische scheisskopf,*" the executioner said as he scowled down at the kill, holstering his P-38 and stalking away on hobnailed jackboots.

At the far end of the broad avenue that ran past the German-held apartment block, more members of the T-Patcher unit who were attacking Wehrmacht emplacements at the base of the mortar-bombarded apartment block received a nasty surprise.

A detachment of the enemy's *flamenwerfer* troopers was hustling up from an armored half-track patrol car that had pulled up under the concealment of a smoke-popping mortar round. Holding the *flamenwerfer*'s nozzle directly in front of him in asbestos-mittened hands, the German pulled the trigger on the flamethrower.

Suddenly there came the terrifying whoosh of flammable gases igniting as the incendiary stream erupted from the flamethrower's nozzle in a thirty-foot plume of hissing, crackling death. The spray of liquid fire caught three T-Patchers of Second Platoon in the sweep of its lethal arc.

Big Butch Bowermeister, Jackass Jacquess and Wheats Dimmock had all been hit. Now they screamed in mortal agony as their flesh caught fire and their fat and muscle tissue began to crackle and pop on their incandescent skeletons. Their dying screams were inaudible above the crackling of the hungry flames that were so hot their eyeballs had begun to melt before the fire even touched them.

The incendiary fluid shot by the *flamenwerfer*s clung to the doomed men's bodies, eating into their flesh and blackening their skeletons. The GIs flopped to the ground, human torches thrashing and flailing before death stilled their convulsions forever.

Newsman Mike Jakeway stood looking on at the awful horror of the flamethrower attack, keeping well distant from the center of the blazing circle of stinking, smoking, sickeningly charbroiled flesh that had been American fighting men only minutes before. He had his Kodak press camera out and was snapping furiously. Jakeway had captured every moment of action in a series of gruesome freeze-frames as the Nazi fire lashed out, a dragon's tongue consuming human flesh in its scorching, crackling maw.

As the charred corpses smoldered on the scorched cobblestones, Jakeway snapped open the camera and pocketed the film roll. He felt pretty shaky, but he knew the film was *pure dynamite*. It would earn him a Pulitzer yet. There was only one problem. How to live long enough to collect it.

24

Whoever had called it "mopping up" had probably never experienced a minute of hard combat life. So thought Sergeant Jaybird Macon to himself as Second Platoon's top kick stood poised on the threshold of combat with his knuckles white with tension around a Mills grenade and its missing cotter pin clenched between his teeth.

The doorway yawned wide, exhaling the musty odors of dry rot, stale urine and decaying masonry. The T-Patchers had fought the Germans to a standstill all along a maze of narrow, twisting alleys in a neighborhood near the Roman Pantheon.

Moving unchallenged beneath eerily silent windows, Private Whitlock had suddenly shouted out.

"Kraut at two o'clock!" he screamed, flattening inside a doorway and raising his rifle.

"You're seein' things, dingaling. There ain't no fucking kraut," one of the T-Patchers told him after the rest of the squad had followed suit and ducked for cover.

"I seen him," Whitlock insisted. "Honest to fucking Christ, I see a kraut, I tell ya! He ducked into that doorway just up ahead."

None of the T-Patchers could tell one way or the other, but if it really was a German Whitlock had spotted, then they were damned if they'd let themselves be set up for an ambush.

Second Platoon moved up cautiously to the suspected doorway into which the figure supposedly vanished. Flanked by his men, their Tommy guns held at the ready, Macon counted to four, hurled the grenade into the dark doorway and tried to flatten himself against the wall tightly. He felt the vibrations coming from the muffled *cuhhh-rump!* of the TNT explosion inside the house.

Lighting a red flare, Macon chucked it inside and came dogtrotting in a pulse beat behind it, gloved hands tightly clenching the foregrip and trigger housing of his Tommy gun as he swept the automatic weapon's muzzle from side to side in the eerie, sputtering red light, alert for the sudden appearance of enemy shooters within the rancid-smelling confines of the smoke-filled interior.

There wasn't a sign of any Germans hiding anywhere within the house, though, Macon noted with relief and allowed his grip to relax somewhat on the burp gun's foregrip.

"Looks clean to me," Macon said to his men, a second too damn soon.

The telltale crack of a high-velocity bullet whipped through the air and struck with a thudding wallop, and the very same instant the doughfoot standing behind Macon clutched his blood-spurting throat.

All he was able to do was make gagging sounds as he desperately tried to stanch the rivering flow of lifeblood from the severed arteries of the usually fatal trachea wound.

"*Pill roller!*" Macon hollered as he hit the dirt, seeing a helmeted, greatcoated figure darting into the hellish shadows cast by the sputtering flare somewhere beyond the open doorway before which he stood.

Macon and Whitlock took off after the sniper just as the medic began an emergency tracheotomy of the wounded dogface, using a fountain pen from his breast pocket to keep the downed man's windpipe open.

The pursuing dogfaces soon found themselves smack up against a blank stone wall. The only exit from that particular room seemed to be along a flight of narrow stone steps that spiraled down into the basement below.

A burst of SMG fire, whining and echoing as bullets ricocheted off stone and left pockmarks in their wake, sent them scrambling back for cover almost as soon as they stepped onto the landing of the basement stairs. From the telltale sound and cadence of the fire, there was no doubt the weapon was a Schmeisser SMG.

Flat against the cold stone wall, sticking out his Tommy gun and firing around the entranceway, Macon raked the interior of the stairwell with a long burst of SMG blind fire. The shots spanged and echoed off the ancient stone walls, pockmarking the stone surface but not doing anything more. Waiting a beat after the echoes of gunfire died away, the T-Patchers were soon hotfooting it down the stairs.

They caught up with their fleeing German quarry a few yards down, at the bottom of the steps. The dome-ceilinged room they were in was lit by caged light bulbs and was full of big oaken casks. Hearing the thud of their boots, the sniper pivoted suddenly from where he crouched near one of the casks, brought up the Schmeisser and squeezed its trigger.

Nothing happened. In the confusion of the chase, the German had forgotten to reload the SMG. To his dismay, the weapon was dry.

"Up with the fuckin' hands!" Macon shouted. At first the man seemed to obey, dropping the Schmeisser and reaching for the ceiling. But as Macon approached a moment later, he dipped his right hand toward his pocket and brought out something that gleamed dangerously in the glare of the naked light bulbs.

But before he could bring his weapon into play, Macon fired the Tommy. The German performed a spastic dance step, then slumped down the side of a big barrel.

A jagged pattern of bullet holes punctured the barrel, which poured a stream of sparkling wine on the dead man's face and onto the flagstone floor of the cellar.

Macon stepped over the body, now drenched with wine. His hand was still inside the pocket of his graygreen coat. Macon kicked the hand out of the pocket with the toe of his combat boot. Clutched within the limp fingers gleamed the object Macon had seen before.

Stooping to pick up the object, Macon saw that it was a kind of locket made out of cheap pewter. Inside the locket were two pictures. One of a smiling blond girl and the other of a crew-cut boy, also blond.

Macon threw the locket on top of the dead man, forcing himself not to think of the photo of his own wife and son that he carried inside his helmet.

"Sorry, pal," Macon told the German, who didn't care anymore.

ONCE THE PERIMETER was declared secure, the sarge and his crew looked around and took stock of their surroundings. As was apparent from the first, the cellar was well stocked with wine. The vino alone was a prize worth dying for.

The brass hats' policy of denying the American fighting man any liquor rations forced him to sell his soul for any undrinkable swill concocted by the Italians and offered under the name "drinking alcohol." The wine cellar was worth its weight in gold.

Suddenly Macon noticed something peculiar that he had not seen before. *Wires.* Wires led from behind one of the wine casks. His next realization was that the German had been crouching just in front of that particular cask when he had spun around to fire at them.

The cellar, Macon realized in a flash, *was booby-trapped.* His heart in his throat, Macon hollered for the other T-Patchers beside him to clear out and hustled up the stairs as fast as he was able.

Diving out through the stone entranceway at the top of the landing, he felt himself picked up by the force of the tremendous explosion as the booby-trapped wine cellar blew straight to hell in a searing ball of fire. The force hurled him out the doorway and into the dusty street.

Amazingly neither Macon nor any of his men were seriously hurt. Their ears rang and they stumbled about dazedly before slumping against a wall while the platoon medic looked them over. They exchanged weak grins, glad to be alive. Being near all that wine sure was nice while it lasted anyway, Macon thought, as he rubbed his ringing ears.

MIKE JAKEWAY DRAGGED on a half-finished Gauloise as he hunched over the beat-up Underwood portable typewriter and banged out the day's press release for his syndicated column, "My View from the Front," which the troops had renamed in less than flattering terms that clearly indicated what they considered his writing to be: garbage.

In his copyrighted newspaper column—which would also become part of the book he was writing about his days spent as a front-line war correspondent, one that he'd already received a fat advance for—Jakeway vividly described the valor of the men of Second Platoon and how the T-Patcher unit had braved untold dangers to overcome a merciless, even inhuman, enemy.

The photos he had turned in to the wire service depicting the use of flamethrowers on the American GIs would undoubtedly score him game points galore with his editor in New York. Jakeway could see a nice, juicy bonus in the cards.

Having banged out, then turned in his story and made sure it was received at the wire service front office on Broadway, Jakeway decided to grab himself a drink at the press club's bar. The long zinc bar was crowded, but Jakeway bellied up to it and flagged down the bartender with a wave of his hand, ordering himself a Scotch and soda.

The flamethrower pics were a major coup, no question about it, he reminded himself as he nursed his drink. They had come out so good you could almost smell the odor of burning flesh. But Jakeway saw rough going ahead. Word had spread like wildfire that the war correspondent was a jinx.

Orders or no orders to the contrary, the T-Patchers were avoiding him as if he were the illegitimate son of Typhoid Mary and Benedict Arnold.

Without their cooperation, his shot at good, human-interest copy was zilch, and Jakeway's editor wanted as much as he could get. Moreover, Jakeway was now beginning to be noticed by the press corps. One major scoop could put him within reach of a big, fat Pulitzer, he had come to realize.

Suddenly Jakeway felt a tap on his shoulder. Turning his head, he found himself looking at a familiar, if not especially well-liked face. The face belonged to one of his esteemed journalistic colleagues.

"I say, old man," Collin Wentworth of the *London Dispatch* said to Jakeway with a smile, "word has it that you're like the bloody Hope Diamond. Bring bad luck to everyone you touch." The Brit newsman signaled to the bartender and received a tall glass of beer.

"Crazy Texans," Jakeway answered by way of response, taking a long pull on the Scotch and stuffing his mouth with small salted pretzels from the bowl sitting atop the bar in front of him. "Don't fucking want to cooperate with the forces of truth and enlightenment."

"Hear, hear," Wentworth said dryly. "We chaps of the fourth estate should get more respect from the buggers at the front, wouldn't you say?"

"Damn fucking right."

"Superstitious lot, those cowboys, I hear tell," Wentworth continued as he nodded with professional sympathy. "Look here, old stick," he went on, "I might have a bit of something right up your alley. Not my cup of tea, so you can have it gratis."

"Yeah, what might that be?" Jakeway asked the Englishman warily. As far as he was concerned, the Brits could sometimes be less trustworthy than the Germans.

"Well, it's rather like this," Wentworth continued dryly. "Rumor has it—and I must stress that this is only a rumor at this point—that the infamous Major Sturmer and a group of SS men are holed up in a stubborn pocket somewhere near the sector your bunch has been operating in. In the event you haven't heard, Sturmer has earned himself quite a reputation as a sadistic killer."

"So?" asked Jakeway. "What of it?" He knew all about Sturmer, all right, who was reputed to have been behind the massacre of a full company of captured GIs whom his SS men were supposedly taking to a POW camp. He didn't see what it had to do with the Brooklyn Bridge, though.

"Well, it would rather be a feather in your cap if you could be in on the capture of this rather dastardly Jerry, wouldn't you say?"

Jakeway understood exactly what the Brit meant. He wondered why he had mentioned the supposed "rumor" and on what information he based his statement.

But the Brit wouldn't say anymore, just that his information came from impeccable sources in the proverbial "high places."

"Thanks," Jakeway told his English opposite number, pushing away from the bar. "I'll remember this."

Wentworth tipped back his beer and ordered another round as he watched the American leave. The OSS chaps who had been using Sturmer as a double agent would owe him for getting the Yanks to clean their bloody sheets.

"I know you will, old man," he said to nobody in particular as he blew the head off the rim of the glass.

25

Not a man in Second Platoon could make sense of why they had been handed this new detail. The T-Patchers all figured it had something to do with the IPS newspaper reporter, Jakeway. As it turned out, they were right. Dead right.

The newsman had pulled strings with the army brass to get the platoon assigned to cleaning out the stubborn pocket of renegade Germans that was still holed up in the western sector of the city, an old neighborhood on the left bank of the Tiber River known as the Tiber Pocket.

Jakeway had long since learned that the brass were pushovers when it came to the press, each CO hankering for publicity the way a hungry spaniel hankers for a bone. The brass in this sector had proven no exception to the universal rule.

The boys in military Intelligence estimated that two battalions of regular troops, interspersed with the odd SS unit and under Major Sturmer's direct control, were entrenched in the embattled sector.

Due in part to the honeycomb of ancient underground passages that ran beneath the cobblestone streets in that old area, Sturmer and his diehards could hold out indefinitely in makeshift bunkers that they had constructed from existing catacomb tunnels, then enlarged and reinforced.

Blood and Glory

Within the protection of such bunkers, they were virtually impervious to even the heaviest Allied carpet bombing. The only way to effectively dislodge them was to take the down-and-dirty approach of sending troops in and flushing the Germans out of their hideyholes in bloody close-quarters fighting.

So Second Platoon moved into the sector, threading their way cautiously through the twisting streets, knowing that their life was just as much in danger even though they were not in a full-scale battle.

Although they hung on by a slender thread, which eventually had to snap, the Germans were not about to give up Rome easily. Those regular troops that were likely to bid for surrender were kept in line by their fanatical SS masters, who were determined to die for their beloved Führer and take all others with them.

Those of the Nazi Wehrmacht who balked were made examples of early on, summarily executed by the SS as a warning to the others. The Texas infantry was again walking into the lion's den, one ruled by Major Heinz Sturmer, desperate but bitterly determined to the end.

FANNING OUT into the mazelike streets of the Tiber Pocket, every member of Second Platoon had the feeling that he was about to stop a bullet. The T-Patchers' presence in the pocket immediately attracted sniper fire, which forced the unit to scurry for cover.

Suddenly a potato masher grenade came crashing down from one of the rooftops many stories above. Its short fuse detonated the German antipersonnel munition in seconds.

A T-Patcher was lifted high into the air by the fierce concussion of the blast, his body thudding down again in a twisted, pitiful heap as the rest of the platoon broke for cover in every direction.

Suddenly the Germans opened up full force with massed automatic fire. Jakeway raised his Kodak press camera, but it was shot out of his hand by a burst of fire. To one side of him, another T-Patcher's head suddenly blew up, and Jakeway felt his face splattered as the headless, faceless body sagged against him, almost knocking him to the ground.

"Oh, sweet Jesus," the reporter whined as he sank to his knees, vomiting up his press club lunch onto his mud-spattered combat boots.

Suddenly he felt something grab his leg. Looking downward as the bullets whined and spanged off the rubble near him, missing him by mere inches, Jakeway saw to his horror that it was the hand of the headless corpse, now clutching him in death.

Motivated by mindless terror, Jakeway pried the fingers of the dead soldier from his foot and half ran, half crawled for cover while tears of panic oozed out of his eyes.

In the disorienting confusion of the sudden firefight, he had become separated from the unit and had immediately lost his sense of direction. After some frantic wondering, the diminishing crack of gunfire and the thudding of mortar shells and grenades from the battle zone told him that he had left the sector.

Finally judging that it was safe to stand again, he rose shakily to his feet. Looking furtively around him, he tried to determine where he was, but the neighborhood was unfamiliar. At least there didn't seem to be any signs of battle activity in the vicinity.

Then he saw that there was a break between two buildings not far to his left, where a flight of crumbling stone stairs led to a higher level of the street, much like the Spanish Steps only far smaller. Figuring that one direction was as good as any—as long as it took him away from the shooting—Jakeway turned and began running toward the stairs.

He didn't want to die. Let all the rest of them die, his mind churned out in panic. *But not him. Not Mike Jakeway. Mike Jakeway he counted for something. He was a reporter. He was writing a book. He had a reason to live.*

Mind spinning like a dervish on a merry-go-round, Jakeway ran up the short stairway toward the safety of the narrow cobblestone street that loomed above him, apparently deserted.

Winded from his run up to the elevated street, Jakeway rested against the wall of a nearby building, wondering where to go next. He could hear his heart thudding savagely inside his heaving chest. Muscles twitched nervously on his face, and cold sweat sheened his cheeks and dribbled down his back.

He had to think of a story to cover his ass. Something that would explain why he had left the battle zone without making it look as though he had turned yellow and run. With any luck, nobody from that platoon would remain alive after the firefight to tell a tale.

And even if there were any survivors, it would be their word against his, and whose word would the brass believe?

Jakeway was beginning to feel better by the minute. In the distance he could hear the sounds of fire being exchanged, of the slow, throaty ratcheting of the German SMGs and the faster tempo of American Tommy guns sending back answering steel, punctuated by the occasional thud of a bursting grenade. But the sounds of battle were still moving no closer to him. In fact, they seemed to be moving steadily away from him. With the sweat drying on his body and his heart slowing to a more normal rate, Jakeway stepped out into the street.

A man in a threadbare corduroy jacket walked toward him, seemingly having appeared from out of nowhere. The man's long, ferretlike face wore an enigmatic expression, neither threatening nor especially comforting. The man simply stood there staring at him. In the second or two that Jakeway looked in his eyes and tried to figure out what he was after, the man pulled a black Webley revolver from his belt and pointed it at Jakeway's stomach.

"Hey, what the—" was all the reporter managed to get out of his mouth before three Magnum rounds tore away most of his abdomen and sent him spinning in a half circle until he collapsed on the street, an unmoving mass in a spreading red pool. As his eyesight dimmed to black, he saw the man stoop over him, felt his hands quickly and expertly rifling through his pockets.

The thief took out the American money in Jakeway's wallet. The press card he threw away, along with the empty wallet. The thief felt good. The things he had stolen from this *brutta faccia* would bring him a small fortune on the black market. His family could at least eat meat for the first time in months.

Damn the Americans, he thought. They had reduced his homeland to rubble, destroyed everything he owned, ruined his wife's morals and turned his children into beggars.

They were worse than the stinking Germans to him, these American pigs. Taking one last look at the bleeding corpse of his victim, the thief spit in the dead man's face and soon disappeared among the ancient ruins of Rome.

STRANDED in the Tiber Pocket, Second Platoon had become pinned down by heavy enemy fire. With their commo gear shot to shit, the unit now found itself cut off in the pocket, surrounded by Sturmer's well-armed and well-deployed soldiers, who had plenty of ammo and nothing much to lose by continuing to fight.

Sergeant Jaybird Macon had watched the newsman scurry away, but there was nothing he could do about Jakeway. Good riddance, he thought to himself. Maybe now that the jinx was gone, at least some members of the platoon stood a snowball's chance of getting back out alive.

Suddenly Macon caught a flicker of movement. BAR-man Hibbard raised his Browning Auto to shoulder height, took aim and was ready to put a round into the scurrying figure, but Macon held him back before he had a chance to squeeze the trigger. It was no German they had seen—that was apparent as the figure drew close.

It was an Italian kid. Dressed in rags, he was an all-too-familiar sight in the bombed-out landscape of Italy. Macon smiled grimly. With his dirty face, ripped, dirty clothes and unkempt hair, he looked just like the cartoon character Topolino.

"I will help you," the waif said to the T-Patchers. "My name Vincenzo," the kid went on. "My mother and father, they killed by Germans. I know way out of here."

"Sure, kid," Macon said back, handing the kid a chocolate bar from his fatigue pocket and watching while it was greedily devoured. Despite having been told the kid's name, Macon knew what he'd privately call him. From now on, the kid's name was Topolino.

26

The warren of tunnels meandered for several miles underneath the cobblestone streets of the old Trans-Tiber district of the city. The section of the tunnel labyrinth into which Second Platoon had now deployed was part of the municipal sewer and storm drainage system.

Dank and dark, the tunnel was filled to knee height with oily, foul-smelling water that had collected as a result of the recent heavy rains drenching the region.

"These tunnels go all underneath Rome," Topolino explained as he led the column of T-Patchers splashing their way along the slime-encrusted flagstones of the ancient Roman sewage channel.

Although manhole covers positioned high up on the tunnel roof at intervals of every hundred yards or so filtered through enough light to see by, anyone unfamiliar with the treacherous twists and turns of the tunnel labyrinth would have soon been hopelessly lost unless they had the benefit of a knowledgeable guide.

"My father, he used to work for city before the Tedeschi—the Germans—take him away. He show me all tunnels in Rome," Topolino continued with pride as he led the T-Patchers surefootedly along one subterranean water channel, the sound of splashes and footfalls echoing off the curved walls of ancient brickwork.

"What happened to your dad?" asked Macon.

Topolino shrugged.

"I don't know," he replied. "Germans took him away to labor camp last year. I have not seen him since."

"And your mother?"

Topolino didn't answer; the kid just looked down at the oily water and started to sob quietly. Macon got the picture, all right. He felt the hot anger rise in his craw like a ball of white lightning.

"It's okay, kid," said Macon, putting his arm protectively around the frail shoulders and realizing that the kid was little more than skin and bones. Changing the subject, he asked, "Who built these tunnels?"

"Old Romans build these tunnels, long time ago," Topolino explained, rubbing tears from his eyes. "Use for sewers. They all empty into Tiber River."

The sergeant was quick to grasp the implications of the street urchin's explanation. If the tunnels ran beneath the streets of the Eternal City, then it was entirely possible that they also gave access to hidden entrances leading up into the cellars of buildings in the neighborhood beneath which they were progressing.

The T-Patcher platoon leader had a sudden recollection of the spiraling stone stairs winding down to the wine cellar. The German soldier they'd shot had tried to duck back down the stairway immediately before the booby-trapped wine casks had gone up with a thunderous explosion.

"Okay, kid," Macon told Topolino, again putting his arm around the orphan's shoulders like a big brother. "Here's what I want you to do." Macon asked the kid if he thought he could lead the platoon to a position that would allow them to resurface at street level somewhere behind the nest of Germans entrenched in the Tiber Pocket.

What Macon had in mind was to use the element of surprise to compensate for the numbers he was lacking to corral the stubborn Germans.

Although the enemy had the advantage of superior manpower, they were also bunched up in their pocket in one vulnerable pile. Concentrated together like this, they had caught themselves in a trap of their own making, much like the fish in the desert ponds that he'd used to catch as a boy in Stone County, Texas.

In the spring the flash rains filled the hollow places in the parched landscape, giving rise to temporary ponds. In these ponds fish spawned by the thousands in a mad frenzy to reproduce before the water was gone again. By high summer the rains had long since vanished and the ponds were fast drying up, leaving the fish stranded and easy prey for beast and man alike.

That's just the way the Germans were now, Macon saw: squirming fish caught in a shrinking pond, just begging to be hooked. Macon aimed to do the Germans right. With luck on their side, he and his T-Patchers were about to have themselves a very good catch.

THE STRONGHOLD WAS located within a complex of subcellar storage chambers beneath what Topolino said was a church on the Piazza Navona. The chambers—originally holding-pens for the Greeks, Nubians and other enslaved peoples—had been enlarged and added to since medieval times and were connected by a branching warren of passageways that had no rhyme or reason.

Macon broke out tear gas grenades and doled them out sparingly to his men, along with gas masks. The platoon didn't have too many of either at its disposal, and the T-Patchers would have to use them carefully, although Macon had no doubt that his men had enough grenades to get the job done.

One of those babies, he knew from past experience as he hefted the black cylindrical canister with white markings covering every side, produced quite a voluminous load of choking tear gas.

Unlike the familiar Mills grenades, the tear gas grenades were cylindrical in shape, although they were armed by the same Bouchon, or "mousetrap," ignitor system.

The grenades did, however, have a slightly shorter detonation delay than the four-and-a-half-second period that the Mills grenades had, so Macon made sure his men knew how to use the gas cans: pitch them, get back and wait until the gas dispersed before moving in.

Since the gas dispersed quickly, the dogfaces could attack in under thirty seconds even without the masks. The whole idea of using the grenades was to flush out the Germans from their hidey-holes and take them prisoner, and Macon hoped the shortage of masks wouldn't be a problem.

MACON AND HIS CREW stood outside the arched approach to one of the enemy bunkers. From inside, they could hear the voices of a couple of men, the sound of chair legs scraping against a bare stone floor and the crunch and slap of hobnailed leather soles accompanying movement within the hideout.

Standing across the archway from the three men in his squad, Macon held up five fingers to indicate that he figured that there were five occupants in the room altogether. As the T-Patchers donned their gas masks, Macon pulled the pin of the tear gas grenade and prepared to chuck it.

Just then a cat ran out of the room, meowing loudly and raising its tail in alarm as it saw the strangers. Macon held back for a moment before making the grenade toss as he heard the rapid slap of boot leather coming right behind the cat.

"Putzi! Come back here, you bad cat," the German called as his crew-cut head, dewlapped throat and beefy shoulders emerged through the arched entranceway.

Spotting the Americans suddenly, his gray eyes went wide, and he began screaming in German about American soldiers inside the bunker. With the element of surprise lost completely, there was no point in using the gas grenade.

Pulling his Colt .45, Macon shot the man right between the eyes and ducked fast as a hailstorm of 9 mm Schmeisser fire flailed through the doorway from within the bunker, a 2-round burst striking Private Willy Black Elk and sending the Indian T-Patcher pinwheeling backward, stone-cold dead before he hit the floor.

Macon chucked the armed tear gas grenade into the room anyway, and stepped quickly to one side as he heard the telltale popping sound of the igniting primer charge followed by the loud hiss of the escaping tear gas.

Despite the fact that the enemy coughed and wheezed inside, they were still pouring autofire from their chattering weapons through the entranceway. Incapacitated now, however, they had no chance of accurately targeting their fire and were only wasting ammo.

Risking a hit from a stray bullet, Macon grabbed his M-1 and went into the room on a half crouch. He quickly dropped below the rising curtain of gas, rolled and started raking the room with side-to-side motions of the death-spitting weapon in his fists. Through the clouds of lazily swirling irritant gas, he could see bodies shimmy and shake as they were ventilated by a fusillade of bullets, then sag dead to the floor.

As he grabbed extra clips from mag pouches on his utility belt, Macon's carbine barked again and again as he was joined by the two surviving members of his squad, who pumped out more blitzing fire, making sure that the rest of the Germans inside the bunker had paid their ultimate dues to the Nazi Party.

Completely taken by surprise everywhere throughout the underground bunker system, the blitzkrieged enemy reacted to the gassing just as Macon had hoped they might.

They had no alternative but to run like hell for the passages leading to the safety of street level. Stationed outside of these, other T-Patchers were waiting to net the catch. As the Germans emerged from the bunker network, the T-Patchers smashed each across the jaw with the butts of their rifles, stripped them of their own weapons and lined them up for capture and interrogation.

BUT SS MAJOR STURMER had other plans for his future. Such ignominy was not to be his fate. The plans involved emptying the safe-deposit boxes in Swiss banks of their millions in plundered loot and retiring to some pleasant Argentinian ranch after the war.

He had long ago scouted out a passageway that he had kept concealed from his men by strategically positioning the ancient stone sarcophagus of a former Roman senator in front of its narrow entrance.

Thanks to a strong streak of claustrophobia, the major had always had an instinctive suspicion of enclosed spaces. Now that long-embraced suspicion had finally paid off.

Racing away from the chaos in the main chambers of the underground hideout, the major shoved aside the heavy sarcophagus and ran into the tunnel, in the process arming himself with a Mauser machine pistol and extra ammo clips that he had secreted away for just such a contingency.

A few yards and about ten minutes later, he was pushing aside the heavy cast-iron circle of a manhole cover set in a Roman back street, then cautiously sticking his head up through the opening and into the pale, waning light of late afternoon.

Sturmer's nostrils twitched as he smelled the acrid odor of cordite fumes and the noxious, rotting stench of the sewers rising from beneath him. But to his delight he also saw that the cobblestone street was deserted from one end to the other. Emerging to shoulder height, he took a better look around him.

The narrow street was flanked on either side by buildings discolored by big-city dirt and grime. The major knew this section of Rome into which he had emerged to be a neighborhood not far from the Farnese Gardens and judged that he was not more than a couple of streets distant from the Tiber River.

With any luck, he could make it back to the line of retreating German troops well ahead of the advancing Americans.

Hauling himself out of the manhole, the major shoved the cast-iron cover back into its niche and began a loping run through the deserted streets on hobnail-booted feet, holding his Mauser machine pistol at the ready in black-gloved hands.

The SS major did not suspect that retribution, in the form of Staff Sergeant Jaybird Macon, was closing in fast directly behind him. Macon had emerged from the one-sided battle underground just in time to see the major ducking into the hole in the catacomb wall and guessed that the big fish was escaping while his minnows were being caught in the net.

Pulling his Colt .45, Macon took aim at the German who was loping down the street, but was too late to draw an accurate bead. The major had already disappeared around the corner of a building with dark ocher walls.

Macon took off after the fleeing German SS officer. It was a big fish and one that he didn't want to let slip away if he could help it.

The SS man would be wanted for interrogation by his CO, there was no doubt about that. Macon was willing to bet that he could provide extremely valuable info on the German military situation in the area, stuff that might help his side in the coming fight to take the north of Italy away from the master race.

"Hold it!" Macon cried out as he spotted the major again after a spring around the corner into a tiny pocket square. Instead of stopping, the major swerved around, whipping the Mauser up toward Macon in a single fluid motion. With a sinking feeling in the pit of his stomach, Macon saw that the SS man was holding a hostage.

It was Topolino.

"I will kill the boy," the German said in clipped but clearly understandable English, drilling the pistol into Topolino's head. "Drop your weapon, Sergeant. Do so now!"

"Nuts to you," Macon yelled back, knowing better than to bargain with an SS man. "You're surrounded," Macon went on, still holding his pistol on Sturmer. "You don't stand a chance. Let the kid go and surrender."

An autofire hailstorm, throwing up yellow sparks on the cobbles at his combat-booted feet, made Macon jump backward for the cover of a nearby fountain as jagged chips of stone cut his face and embedded themselves in his arm. The German had given him his answer all right, speaking a language that he knew best.

As a parting shot, the man turned and coldbloodedly shot Topolino through the heart. The slight body was knocked off its feet and flung two feet into the air by the impact of the point-blank parabellum burst, then crashed to the cobblestone street in a tangled, blood-oozing heap.

Whirling around, the killer made a beeline for the cover of a large statue nearby, then disappeared down an alleylike street that ran off in a straight line just beyond it. Macon recovered his orientation and pursued his fleeing quarry down the street.

Stopping as he reached Topolino's body, Macon put his ear to the boy's chest and listened for a heartbeat. A snarl of outrage turning his face into a baleful mask, Macon closed Topolino's sightless eyes, then took off after his murderous quarry.

27

Macon chased the major into an ancient amphitheater that stood in a piazza to which a number of streets led in a circle.

The place was called the Theater of Marcellus, built originally by the Roman emperor Augustus in honor of his son-in-law and was the model for the larger Colosseum, although Macon didn't know this. All he knew was that the man he sought had gone inside there, and so would he.

As the T-Patcher entered the cool darkness of the arched passageways that honeycombed the ancient colonnaded stone galleries of the amphitheater's interior, he was temporarily blinded as his eyes refocused to accommodate the shadows. In that instant Macon heard a telltale click somewhere on his right and instinctively ducked.

Had he reacted a microsecond more slowly, the Mauser burst of 9 mm parabellum rounds that the major sent whipsawing in his direction would have blown his head clean off.

Instead, the machine pistol's deadly burst sent chips of pulverized limestone flying in his face. Cut just above the eyebrow, Macon wiped blood from his cheeks and the bridge of his nose.

His eyes now having become accustomed to the darkness, Macon hurled answering .45-caliber fire at the SS officer, who crouched for cover behind a fluted stone column. The heavy-caliber bullets fired by the Colt sizzled by the major's head as the big gun bucked in Macon's fist until finally its clip ran dry.

The major had enough sense to break and run while Macon reloaded. With the survival instincts of a big cat, he darted from shadow to sunlight, using the walls and the massive stone columns and statuary for cover.

The hammer cocked and a round freshly chambered, Macon was forced to hold his fire, unable to draw a solid bead on his fast-moving target. He knew that the major's strategy was to make him use up his ammo reserves if he could, then blow the American away at his convenience. The T-Patcher NCO wasn't about to let himself be suckered that way, though.

The game of lethal hide-and-seek continued, with Macon giving chase across the ancient killing ground. World War II might still be going on, but within the all-embracing silence of the ancient Roman amphitheater, two men were locked in a timeless contest from which only a single combatant would ultimately emerge alive.

The game of terminal tag was broken by the sudden appearance of the German from beneath the rim of the bowl of the amphitheater's multitiered gallery.

As he popped up from a crouched position between the stone slabs that had served as benches for the cheering crowd of long ago, the Mauser in his hand splatted an obscenely razzing tongue of jetting yellow fire, sending a broadside of hot Krupp steel whizzing at Macon.

The American felt the heat of the glowing steel-jacketed parabellums zipping past his shoulder as he leaped back behind the safety of the stone parapet he'd stood upon.

Answering .45-caliber fire roared from the bucking Colt in Macon's fist, but the SS major was as fast as he was tricky. Macon's hailstorm of bullets scythed harmlessly through thin air, a pulse beat behind the artfully dodging enemy.

Keeping one step ahead of Macon's tracking Colt, the major vaulted a stone balustrade, his groundward plunge cushioned by the thick leather soles of his hobnailed jackboots. He landed on his haunches, his well-toned thigh muscles absorbing the shock of impact, and whirled in place to jab the Mauser in the T-Patcher's direction, a snarl of contempt on his lips.

The major had expected the sudden surprise movement to leave his enemy exposed and a sitting duck for a lethal Mauser put-away burst. But he had been disappointed, and an expression of dismay crossed his cold, patrician features.

Sighting over the Mauser's barrel, the major tracked the weapon from side to side, but saw nothing except for the almost unearthly emptiness of the sun-dappled stone galleries. They yawned back at him as if to mock him. The American was nowhere to be seen.

It was the sudden flutter of a surprised pigeon's wings that made the German tuck quickly sideways and roll out of the stream of deadly lancing Colt fire as Macon opened up from the protection of a rectangular stone entranceway opening onto the gravel-strewn floor of the Roman hippodrome. From these entranceways Christians had been thrown before lions, and gladiators dueled for the entertainment of bloodthirsty Roman nobility and plebeians alike in centuries gone by.

The major rose to his full height on jackbooted feet. He took the measure of the American T-Patcher who now confronted him within the circular killing ground, and the malevolent sneer returned to the Nazi's angular face.

The American was as tall as he, with broad shoulders and the demeanor of a campaign-hardened warrior. The differences in their rank were meaningless under the circumstances.

The major was aware that he faced an equal on the field of combat. Here was an opponent who had every right to command his complete respect. The pitched firefight had resulted in a standoff, the major knew. Both men now had each other covered with their respective weapons. Neither could hope to overcome the other as things presently stood.

"My name is Heinz," the major shouted at Macon in the same clear English he had spoken earlier. The Mauser in his hand remained level with the T-Patcher's heart zone. "What are you called?"

"Jaybird's the name," Macon shouted back, hearing his own amplified voice bouncing and echoing off the ancient stone galleries as the boom and thunder of the distant guns rumbled ominously beyond the encircling columns of weathered ancient marble.

"I find it ironic," the major began, "that we stand here today as we do. Two thousand years before, captured warriors from Germanic hill tribes were dragged to this arena as gladiators for the entertainment of their Roman conquerors. Perhaps our remote ancestors fought and died on this very same patch of ground."

"Yeah, so what?" Macon asked.

The major told himself to remember that this was an American he was addressing. As worthy an opponent as he might be, the Americans were uncultured boors, men whose ancestors had been the outcasts of Europe. Major Sturmer realized that he could not hope to make his thoughts understood to such a one as this brutish, uneducated Texan.

"Just this," the SS major replied. "This amphitheater is the playground of Mars, the Roman god of war. Therefore, I propose that we settle our differences man-to-man, as did the ancient gladiators who stood this bloodstained ground long before our time. I propose, further, that we fight by other means."

To underscore his meaning, the major flung down his Mauser to the dusty ground. It landed at his feet with a hollow clunk, and he kicked it away from him.

Macon watched the German through half-slitted eyes.

"Suits me fine," he said finally, tossing the Colt automatic away from him and hearing it clatter somewhere in the stone bleachers behind and to one side of where he stood. When he got right down to it, Macon liked this arrangement a whole lot better. The satisfaction of doling out justice with his bare knuckles would be even better than doing him with a gun.

Having thrown away his weapon, the major drew a more ancient weapon. He pulled the long SS dagger from its oiled scabbard slowly, confidently. He unsheathed the dagger in the manner of a man used to fighting with knives and right at home in hand-to-hand combat.

In point of fact, he was a master of the art of knife fighting. Heinz Sturmer had carried the dagger proudly since his graduation from the SS academy at Bad Tolz.

The long dagger's handle of burnished black stone bore the twin lightning flashes of the Nazi Shutzstaffel, or SS. Beneath it was emblazoned the sardonically grinning *totenkupf,* or death's-head, of the elite SS troops. On the flat of the long, wickedly sharp blade was inscribed the motto of the SS unit to which the Major belonged. The motto read: *Meine Ehre Heisst Treue*—My Honor Is Loyalty.

In sharp contrast with the Nazi, the knife that Macon pulled from his side scabbard bore no special insignia on its haft or martial inscription on its blade. It was standard Army issue. No better, no worse. But the long combat dagger gleamed as menacingly in the T-Patcher's hands as the Nazi's fancy blade did.

Weapons flashing in the sun, the two men cautiously approached each other, beginning to circle like big jungle cats.

Moving first, the German took a swipe that was calculated more to take the American's measure than to actually cut him. The American reacted with superb quickness, deftly sidestepping the vicious, glittering arc aimed at his midsection.

Macon didn't take the sucker bait and attempt to stab the major, who had been prepared to pivot and plunge the dagger into the American's unprotected flank on the follow-through—had the Yank been foolhardy enough to take the fool's gambit he had offered.

"Very good," the major growled with grudging admiration at his enemy's resourcefulness. He pivoted to face the American again. "You have earned my congratulations." Although breathing heavily and with his brow filmed lightly with sweat, he was far from winded.

Quick and deadly, the Nazi lunged again, cold steel glinting in a lethal arc. This time it was no mere diversionary feint. It was for real, with the death strike angled in low and the blade turned inward to mangle and wound.

The path of the knife's cutting edge would sweep it in toward Macon's heart region, just below the shoulders. If the American managed somehow to block the thrust, then the knife would still inflict crippling harm. Once his opponent was paralyzed, Sturmer could strike again, this time more leisurely, yet to still more deadly effect.

The major had not reckoned with two things, however. The first was that Macon knew enough not to trust the German to play by Queensbury rules, and the second was that Macon had graduated from grade school knowing three *R*s and a *K*—for knife fighting. Judging from his opponent's position as he went into his vicious death strike, Macon had been able to figure out his strategy and knew just how to counter it.

Pivoting his body and simultaneously ducking to a half crouch, the T-Patcher sergeant stepped quickly beneath the deadly sweep of the knife, hearing it whistle past his ear. At that precise instant, Macon thrust his own dagger forward in a straight line, using the power in his arm to stick it up into the Nazi's unprotected entrails with all his might.

The man grunted with pain as the blade sheared through his stomach and came out through his kidney, its tip shiny with thick blood. Yet Macon's move had also left him open to a counterattack. With a savage curse on his lips, Sturmer drove the blade of his SS dagger down into the muscular portion of his enemy's arm.

Hot blood spurted in thick, pulsing jets over both combatants, who now circled each other with the slow, deliberate movements of antagonists who have seriously wounded each other, trying not to show the extent of the searing pain that threatened to overwhelm them both at any moment.

"You are very good," Sturmer said, grimacing from his wound as he wiped blood from his eyes. Quickly feinting right, he thrust his dagger once more into the opening he saw to Macon's rib cage, inflicting a slicing cut on Macon's side.

Ignoring the fiery pain in his side, Macon reacted quickly, kicking the mortally wounded German in the ribs and sending the SS dagger flying from his weakened grasp. Sturmer swayed drunkenly and then collapsed to the ground a few moments later. Covered with his own blood, Macon stood reeling over the Nazi. Breathing in ragged gasps, he held his own dagger poised for striking as the world before his eyes began to run like melting butter.

"Get up," he said, weaving from side to side as he loomed over the prostrate German, struggling to keep from blacking out himself.

"What is preventing you?" the major asked, holding his blood-gushing belly wound. "Finish it now. I would have done the same."

"Don't think I don't want to." Even now, facing a dying man, Macon detested the sight of the Nazi's face. But he didn't want to sink as low as his enemy was. If he allowed himself to, then Macon knew that he would still have lost the fight. "Get up," he repeated.

As Macon reached down to pull the German to his feet, he was suddenly blinded by a handful of gravel flung into his face. As the major had gone down, he had reached out and grabbed up the fistful of small stone pellets, hiding his hand beneath his body. Macon spluttered curses and clawed at his injured face, letting go of his knife by reflex action.

The Nazi saw the dull flint of the blued metal finish of his discarded Mauser machine pistol lying a couple of feet from where he lay. Jumping to one side in a final spurt of ebbing strength, he grabbed for the gun and picked it up.

By the time Macon's vision cleared, he saw that the Nazi was clutching the Mauser. Sturmer held the machine pistol on him in a two-handed shooter's grip. He knew that although the severely injured man was staggering back and forth, at such close range he couldn't miss even if he tried.

"You were stupid," the major growled as he chambered a round. "Stupid and weak. You do not deserve to live."

Then he squeezed the trigger.

Macon was lifted off his feet by the tremendous force of the explosion, deafened by the boom of thunder that filled his head and sent him spinning off into a void of total blackness.

When he opened his eyes a moment later and scrambled to a kneeling position, he saw the twenty-foot bomb crater that now occupied the spot where the German had stood only moments before. The stray artillery shell had decided the issue for both of them.

THE T-PATCHERS MARCHED a long column of German prisoners out of the Tiber Pocket. Riding behind them in a captured German staff car was Second Platoon's sergeant, now sporting bandages where he'd been wounded by the major's blade.

"Cap'n," Macon said to Murch Cody, who awaited the platoon's arrival, "we're officially turning over these prisoners to you."

"What happened to the reporter?" Cody wanted to know as he gave the once-over to the disheveled-looking ranks of beaten men who had believed not very long before that the German army was invincible.

"Well, sir," Macon replied to his CO, "I guess you'd have to call him missing in action." Cody understood exactly what the sergeant meant. Whatever had happened to Jakeway, he'd probably deserved what he'd got.

"Nice going, Sergeant," Cody informed him. "I'll report the newsman's disappearance to General Hoagland. It's too bad, but these things happen in war."

"Yeah," Macon told Cody, "it sure is too damn bad about Jakeway," and shifted the jeep into gear.

28

With the Germans finally out of their hair, the Italians were of a mind for celebration. It seemed as though the entire population of Rome had taken to the streets in droves as the triumphant Allied armies marched into town by way of the Forum of the Caesars, right through the arch of Constantine.

As night fell, colored party lights were strung out all across the city, and people felt like celebrating now that the misery was over.

Easy Company's commander, Murch Cody, well knew that the festive mood would wear off soon enough. For now, he was content to ride with it. But he knew it took more than a day to repair the devastation and misery caused by war.

Like Cody and his men, the top Army brass had been naive when it came to understanding how the German military mind worked and how the German military machine went about fighting a war.

They had landed troops on the beachheads of Salerno and Anzio, believing that the enemy needed no softening up, that the sheer might of their fighting men and war matériel would be enough to defeat the enemy, and they had been proven wrong on both occasions.

At Anzio, Ike and the joint chiefs had not profited from the hard-won knowledge that they had gained at Salerno. There had been some preinvasion bombardment of enemy holdouts, but again American troops had arrived in the combat zone facing troops who were intact in well-fortified positions, ready to cut them down.

Again, the price of neglectfulness had been paid for with rivers of human blood.

Monte Cassino had been another mistake, for the Germans had never in the first place held the monastery at its peak as so many had insisted. But the bombing that had destroyed it had at least demonstrated that Eisenhower and Montgomery were now determined to err on the side of caution.

When Rome's time came to face the Allied judgment call, the lesson about the Germans had been finally learned. No longer would the Allied brass allow their men to sacrifice themselves on the bloody altar of military indecisiveness. No longer would German mortar pits, machine-gun emplacements and troops holding the high ground welcome men who fought from a position of tactical inferiority.

This time the B-29s had been sent out, the bombs dropped and the arrogant Nazi minions who held Rome pounded to near insanity by air support before any troops ever went in.

It was too bad about the Italians, Cody mused, but it had to be done. In the end Cody felt vindicated. His men had taken the city away from a despicable enemy.

And so it was that Cody didn't mind the new assignment that Major General Hoagland had handed him and some of his T-Patchers. Bomb-clearing duty wasn't the most glamorous job in the Army, but it was a job that needed doing. The problem was in getting men to volunteer.

Bomb-clearing duty wasn't just unglamorous; it was also highly dangerous, which is why Cody was tooling his battle-scarred jeep down toward the company replacement depot, or "repple-depple," at the edge of the city to try to "volunteer" himself some good men for a dirty job.

Men finding themselves penned up in such a place were generally more amenable to any opportunity to escape their MP guardians than any other soldier. Cody stopped the jeep and walked toward the compound.

"Get a load of this, Sarge."

One of Fifth Platoon's men handed Lou Jack a newspaper just arrived from the States. It was a rare edition—rare because it was one that was fairly recent. The edition contained the final column of the late, lamented Mike Jakeway.

By coincidence, the column told of the brave exploits of their own platoon. The only problem with the story was that nothing that Jakeway had written about had actually ever taken place. Every word was a masterpiece of bullshit.

The editorial fine print at the bottom of the column stated that the newspaper staff lamented that Jakeway was killed in action shortly after turning in the column and referred readers to the obituary appearing later in the same edition.

"Guy looks uglier in this photo than he did in real life," Lou Jack commented as he read the obituary in the back pages, full of praise from Jakeway's fellow journalists and mentioning that a book of his collected war stories was to be published soon by Fisk, Dunbar and Fisk of Cleveland, Ohio, then handed back the paper.

Just then, a big transport chugged into the company repple-depple. It was the truck that would take him home by way of Naples. Hearing his name called, Lou Jack picked up his pack full of gear and hopped on board.

For Lou Jack, this was the end of his second and final hitch in the Army. The truck would be carrying him away from Rome, back to the States. With his demobilization pay, he figured on starting some kind of business, maybe opening up a burger joint somewhere along one of the new interstates.

But a moment after the rig got rolling, Lou Jack experienced a sudden change of heart. Call it intuition, but Lou Jack realized then and there that he wasn't meant to go home. Not yet, anyway.

"Hey, driver, stop this rig, willya," Lou Jack hollered out, his fist hammering repeatedly on the top of the truck's cab. As the truck lurched to a sudden halt to the accompaniment of the shouts and curses of disgruntled dogfaces eager to start their journeys Stateside, Lou Jack jumped off and started walking back into the replacement depot, his cigar stuck in the corner of his mouth, his dress cap canted cockily back on his crew-cut head.

Damned if he wasn't going to hang around long enough to see Berlin get kicked right in its Axis before they shipped him back to Amarillo and that dingaling burger joint.

The banged-up jeep that pulled up just behind the again-departing transport was a familiar sight to Lou Jack Claymore. Murch Cody leaned out the driver's side, a big smile on his face.

"I thought you were supposed to be on that transport, Sergeant," he said.

"Yeah, I suppose I was," Lou Jack answered, omitting the "sir." Cody watched the truck disappear beyond a dip in the road, leaving nothing but a shimmer of heat and a cloud of yellow dust in its wake.

"Need a lift somewhere, Sergeant?" Cody asked Lou Jack. "If you're interested in reenlisting, I can put the paperwork right through."

Lou Jack wasn't born yesterday. When any officer, even a T-Patcher officer, sounded that goddamn accommodating, he knew that there had to be a major catch to the deal somewhere.

"What's the duty, Cap'n?" he asked skeptically.

"Bomb-clearing detail," Cody returned without missing a beat.

Lou Jack stood and regarded the captain with narrowed eyes, then shook his head from side to side, gave out a snort of laughter and finally hopped aboard the jeep.

"Let's go, Cap'n," he said as Cody put the pedal to the floorboards and shot the jeep out of the repple-depple into the sun-drenched, bombed-out wreckage of the city. He had come too far and fought too hard to say goodbye to it just yet.

Bolan's on a one-man mission to avert international disaster when a group of Irish terrorists plan the unthinkable... the assassination of the queen.

DON PENDLETON's
MACK BOLAN.

BLOCKADE

The Curran Brigade—a new faction of Irish freedom fighters—are actually ruthless terrorists using patriotism as a front for their diabolical plans. It's up to Mack Bolan to stop the madness before the horrifying conspiracy is realized... and puts the world at war.

Available now at your favorite retail outlet, or order your copy by sending your name, address, zip or postal code along with a check or money order for $5.25 (includes 75¢ postage and handling) payable to Gold Eagle Books to:

In the U.S.
3010 Walden Ave.
P.O. Box 1325
Buffalo, NY 14269-1325

In Canada
P.O. Box 609
Fort Erie, Ontario
L2A 5X3

Please specify book title with your order.
Canadian residents add applicable federal and provincial taxes.

SB22-1A

AGENTS

The action-packed new series of the DEA.... Sudden death is a way of life at the drug-enforcement administration—in an endless full-frontal assault on America's toughest war: drugs. For Miami-based maverick Jack Fowler, it's a war he'll fight to the end.

TRIGGER PULL
PAUL MALONE

In TRIGGER PULL, a narc's murder puts Fowler on a one-man vengeance trail of Miami cops on the take and a Bahamian kingpin. Stalked by Colombian gunmen and a hit team of Metro-Dade's finest, Fowler brings the players together in a win-or-lose game where survival depends on the pull of a trigger.

Available now at your favorite retail outlet, or order your copy by sending your name, address, zip or postal code along with a check or money order for $4.25 (includes 75¢ postage and handling) payable to Gold Eagle Books to:

In the U.S.
Gold Eagle Books
3010 Walden Ave.
Box 1325
Buffalo, NY 14269-1325

In Canada
Gold Eagle Books
P.O. Box 609
Fort Erie, Ontario
L2A 5X3

Please specify book title with your order.
Canadian residents please add applicable federal and provincial taxes.

AGI-1

TAKE 'EM NOW

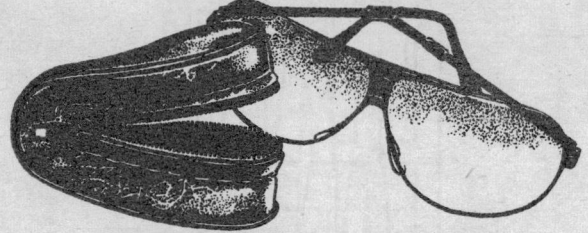

FOLDING SUNGLASSES FROM GOLD EAGLE

Mean up your act with these tough, street-smart shades. Practical, too, because they fold 3 times into a handy, zip-up polyurethane pouch that fits neatly into your pocket. Rugged metal frame. Scratch-resistant acrylic lenses. Best of all, they can be yours for only $6.99.
MAIL YOUR ORDER TODAY.

Send your name, address, and zip code, along with a check or money order for just $6.99 + .75¢ for delivery (for a total of $7.74) payable to Gold Eagle Reader Service.
(New York residents please add applicable sales tax.)

Remove from pouch...

unfold once...

Gold Eagle Reader Service
3010 Walden Avenue
P.O. Box 1396
Buffalo, N.Y. 14240-1396

unfold twice...

and they're ready to wear.

Offer not available in Canada.

In the Deathlands,
everyone and everything is fair game,
but only the strongest survive....

Latitude Zero

Heading west toward the nearest gateway, Ryan Cawdor and his band of post-holocaust survivors are trapped in a nightmare when a deal necessary for their survival pits them against Ryan's oldest enemy—a sadistic, ruthless man who would stop at nothing to get his hands on Ryan Cawdor.

Available in April at your favorite retail outlet, or order your copy by sending your name, address, zip or postal code along with a check or money order for $5.25 (includes 75¢ postage and handling) payable to Gold Eagle Books to:

In the U.S.
3010 Walden Ave.
P.O. Box 1325
Buffalo, NY 14269-1325

In Canada
P.O. Box 609
Fort Erie, Ontario
L2A 5X3

Please specify book title with your order.
Canadian residents please add applicable federal
and provincial taxes.

DL12-1